THE LIBRARY DETECTIVE RETURNS

Former Homicide cop Hal Johnson now works as 'library fuzz' — spending his days chasing down overdue books, stolen volumes, and owed fines. He doesn't miss life in the fast lane. But his police training and detective instincts still prove necessary in the bibliographic delinquency division. For such apparently innocuous peccadillos on the part of borrowers often set Hal on the trail towards uncovering greater crimes: fraud, theft, drug-smuggling, arson — and even murder . . .

D1151263

Books by James Holding
in the Linford Mystery Library:

THE LIBRARY DETECTIVE

JAMES HOLDING

THE LIBRARY DETECTIVE RETURNS

Complete and Unabridged

LINFORD
Leicester

First published in the United States of America

First Linford Edition
published 2017

A catalogue record for this book is available
from the British Library.

ISBN 978–1–4448–3491–8

Published by
F. A. Thorpe (Publishing)
Anstey, Leicestershire

Set by Words & Graphics Ltd.
Anstey, Leicestershire
Printed and bound in Great Britain by
T. J. International Ltd., Padstow, Cornwall

This book is printed on acid-free paper

1

The Henchman Case

My first stop on Monday morning was at a run-down duplex apartment in the West End, the abode of a Mr. Jefferson Cuyler. I parked my car at the curb under a plane tree that was shedding its bark in shabby strips, dodged through a cluster of preschoolers who, with intent faces, were playing some mysterious street game, and mounted the four steps to the door of Mr. Cuyler's residence.

Our records showed Mr. Cuyler was several weeks late in returning six books he had borrowed from the public library. He had neither renewed them nor heeded our postcard of reminder. So I had come in person to collect them.

That's part of my job. I'm Hal Johnson, book collector — or, as my former boss Lieutenant Randall of Homicide calls me, 'library fuzz.' I'm employed by the public

1

library to chase down overdue and stolen library books. That sounds like a simple job, right? Well, it isn't. Not when you consider that in many public libraries (including ours) more than twenty percent of all the new books placed on the shelves vanish after less than a year. *Every* year. We're doing everything we can to cut down on this enormous loss. We're installing book detection systems, taking on extra guards, refusing public admission to certain stacks of out-of-print or rare books, and hiring ex-cops like me to shove fingers in the dyke.

Anyway, there I was on Mr. Cuyler's cramped front porch. I rang the bell. After a minute, the door was opened by one of the handsomest men I've ever seen in my life. He was tall and relatively slender, a year or two past sixty at a guess. His iron-grey hair was crisp and inclined to curl although it was cut short. His complexion was fresh and healthy under a moderate suntan. His features were almost classically regular. And his eyes were cobalt blue, their gaze so candid and friendly that you felt you could trust him with your life if need be.

He said, 'Yes?'

I introduced myself and showed him my ID card. 'Are you Jefferson Cuyler?'

He nodded.

'I've come for your overdue library books,' I explained. 'You've kept them out too long without renewal. So you owe us some fines.'

'I know it,' he said, his friendly eyes not cooling in the slightest. 'I'm sorry, I've been away for a spell. I meant to bring them back today.' He gave me a half-smile. 'They're here. Come on in.'

He led me into his living room and pointed to a battered coffee table. The six library books made a neat stack on one corner of it.

The books were all that was neat in the room. Everything else looked like the aftermath of a cyclone. Somebody had jerked up the faded carpet and tossed it into a crumpled heap in a corner. The cushions and upholstery of the sofa and chair had been slashed in half a dozen places with a sharp knife. The pictures were torn from their hooks, the draperies from their rods. A large TV lay on its side, shattered. The contents of the room's only closet had been dumped on the floor in disarray. Through an old-fashioned archway, I could see that Mr. Cuyler's dining room had been given similar treatment. And probably his bedroom and kitchen as well.

'What the hell happened here?' I asked.

His blue eyes brooded on the confusion around us. 'Well, as I said, I've been away — fishing. This is what I found when I got home an hour ago. Somebody broke in through the back window.'

'Have you called the police?'

'I guess I'd better, hadn't I?' He gave me a funny slanting look accompanied by a wry smile. 'I've been checking out the mess. Lucky your library books weren't lost in the shuffle.'

I gazed around me. 'These weren't your ordinary friendly neighborhood burglars, Mr. Cuyler. I hope you realize that.'

He shrugged. 'I haven't had any previous experience.'

'Well, I have. And I've never seen a more thorough job. Whoever turned the

4

place over was looking for something special, I'd say.'

Cuyler's handsome features shaped themselves into an expression of bafflement. 'I don't know what it could be. It's not as though I own the Hope Diamond.'

'What's missing?' I asked. It wasn't my business any more, but old habits die hard.

'Nothing,' Cuyler said, 'as far as I can tell. Nothing here worth stealing, anyway.'

'You're forgetting my library books,' I said, keeping it light. 'Did you know that it would cost the library an average of fourteen bucks apiece to replace these six books on the shelves if anything happened to them?'

'I had no idea a library book could be so valuable,' he said. His cobalt eyes mirrored a new, nameless emotion for a brief instant. Anger? Uncertainty? Amusement? Triumph? Maybe a little of all of them. It wasn't until later that I recalled he'd said 'could be' instead of the more natural 'was.' 'How much of a fine do I owe?' he asked.

I told him, and finished checking the

titles of his books against my list while he got his money and paid me. 'Thanks,' I said. 'I'm sorry to bother you when you've got all this on your mind.' I gestured at the chaos of the room.

'Forget it,' he said. 'You couldn't have come at a more opportune time.'

Politely, he saw me to the door.

★   ★   ★

That was Monday. The next time I heard anything about Cuyler, he was dead.

Lieutenant Randall telephoned me at the library during my lunch break on Friday.

'Listen, Hal,' he said, 'do me a favor.'

'What is it?'

'A book called *The Henchman*. By somebody named Eugene Stott?'

'Yeah?'

'You got it in the library?'

'Yeah.'

'You know the book?'

'Yeah. At least, the title rings a bell. It was on one of my overdue lists earlier this week.'

'Good. Find out if it's in or out, will

you? And if it's in, hold it for me.'

'For what?' I said. 'You know you can't reserve a book over the telephone, Lieutenant. Why are you interested in it?'

His voice held a note of weariness. 'It may be a 'clue' in a murder I'm working on.' He put audible quotation marks around the word *clue*. 'So move your tail, O.K.? Call me back at this number.' He gave me a telephone number.

I moved my tail. Ten minutes later, I called him back and told him that we had two copies of *The Henchman* circulating from the main library. Copy number one was on the shelves in its assigned place when I looked, and I'd taken it aside for him. Copy number two had been borrowed on Tuesday by a lady named Carolyn Seaver.

Randall hesitated. 'Could you drop the one you have off at Headquarters for me?'

'Sure, Lieutenant. On my way home. No trouble.'

'Thanks. It may give us a lead, Hal. God knows we need one.'

I had a cold flash of intuition. 'Where are you now?'

'West End. Why?'

'I'm wondering if your murder victim could be a man named Jefferson Cuyler,' I said.

Dead silence. Finally, 'Still a show-off, aren't you? How'd you guess that?'

'He's the guy I collected the *The Henchman* from on Monday. I remember it now. He was a handsome — '

'He's far from handsome now.' Randall paused. 'Could you bring that book out *here*, Hal? If you saw this guy on Monday, you may be able to help us.'

'Give me ten minutes,' I said.

'I'll give you fifteen,' Randall growled. 'You're a private citizen now, remember? You can't break the speed laws with impunity anymore.'

'Yes, Lieutenant,' I said humbly. He's never forgiven me for leaving Homicide to become a sissy library cop.

★   ★   ★

When I got to Cuyler's duplex, I told Jimmy Coogan, the Homicide cop on the door, that Randall wanted to see me.

Coogan, an old buddy of mine at the department, passed me inside with a friendly sneer about my present line of work.

I don't know what I was expecting to see on this second visit to Cuyler's house — maybe the same scene of chaos as the first time. Anyway, I was a little bit surprised at how quickly the place had been returned to a condition of normal bachelor neatness. The pictures and draperies had been rehung, the closet contents hidden away again, the rug replaced, the TV set repaired. Even the slashed sofa and chair had been treated to ready-made slipcovers that hid their knife wounds.

Lieutenant Randall was sitting in the chair. 'Come in, Hal. You got that book?'

I held it out to him. He took it without a word and leafed carefully through it. Then, with a frustrated shake of his head, he put the book aside, fixed his spooky yellow eyes on me, and said, 'Tell me about seeing Cuyler on Monday.'

'I can't tell you much. It was just a routine call for overdue books. Except that this house was a howling mess when I arrived. Somebody had broken in and been through it with a fine-tooth comb while Cuyler was away fishing.'

'I already got that much from Robbery's report. Nothing was stolen, they say.'

'Well, it wasn't just a casual break-in, Lieutenant. Somebody was looking for something special. Couldn't Cuyler give Robbery any hints about who or what?'

'Apparently not. But it stands out a mile that Cuyler's murder ties in with it somehow.'

I nodded. 'Who found him?'

'His once-a-week cleaning woman. She has a key, and tripped over Cuyler when she walked in at seven-thirty. The M.E. guessed he'd been dead less than seven hours when he was here at eight-thirty. So it happened early this morning, probably, not long after midnight. And we haven't got anything on it yet. Zilch. None of the neighbors saw or heard anything out of the way last night or this morning. And the killers didn't leave calling cards.' He sighed. 'They never do.'

'Who *was* Cuyler, anyway?' I asked.

'Cuyler? Jefferson Rhine Cuyler, born and brought up in the East End, a widower for eight years, sixty-three years old, retired with a bad heart from Crane Express over a year ago, took early Social Security and has been living here alone. He had only one living relative, out of town somewhere.'

'He must have had something more valuable than a distant relative,' I said.

Randall said, 'That seems obvious. That's why I asked you to bring the book. Whoever killed Cuyler beat the hell out of him before he died. Cuyler had three broken ribs, multiple bruises all over, marks on his wrists and ankles where he'd been tied up. And his face was a disaster.'

I remembered Cuyler's good looks and his warm friendly manner, and thought that he wasn't the type to withstand torture for very long without cracking. Especially with a bad heart.

Randall seemed to sense my thoughts. 'It's possible his killer didn't intend him to die. He may just have been trying to get Cuyler to talk. But the beating killed him, the medical examiner thinks. Caused heart arrest.' Randall rubbed a big hand over his face and I could hear his whisker-bristles rasp. 'It must have been somebody he knew. There wasn't any sign of forced entry this time.'

'The cleaning woman has a key, you said.'

'She couldn't tie up a grown man and break his ribs with punches. She's seventy years old, four feet ten, and weighs ninety-six pounds!'

I grinned. 'Just suggesting a possibility,' I said.

He grunted.

I pointed to *The Henchman*, precariously balanced on the arm of Randall's chair. 'So what did you want that for?'

In reply, Randall took an envelope from his pocket, and from it he carefully extracted a sheet of unlined memo paper, which he held out for me to see. 'Ned Jordan found this when he was dusting for fingerprints. It's the top sheet of a memo pad Cuyler kept beside his telephone.'

I leaned closer. The dusting powder had revealed faint impressions of handwriting on the paper's surface — indentations obviously made by a sharp pencil or pen pressing on the sheet above it. I could make out the smudged words quite easily:

The Henchman Eugene Stott
Public Library

I looked at Randall. He nodded, somewhat sheepishly. 'It's a chance in a million, I know that. But the handwriting doesn't match Cuyler's. So it might be that Cuyler's killers — or one of them — wrote the words on the memo pad.'

'Making a note of information he'd beaten out of Cuyler, you mean?'

'Could be. Maybe the book stuff was all he got out of Cuyler before he cashed in. But then, I couldn't be that lucky. Your damned book doesn't seem to give us a thing.'

'Let me look.'

Randall passed me the book. I examined it carefully. Nothing. 'Maybe this isn't the copy Cuyler had.'

Randall said, 'Check it, O.K.?'

I went to Cuyler's phone and called Ellen, the girl on the check-out desk at the library. I'm hoping she'll marry me someday. I usually propose to her every time I see her. 'Listen, Ellen,' I said, 'find out which of our two copies of *The Henchman* by Eugene Stott I brought back on Monday from our card-holder, Jefferson Cuyler, will you?'

She recognized my non-courting voice. 'Hold on,' she said, all business. In a minute or two she was back on the line and informed me that copy number two of *The Henchman* was the one that Jefferson Cuyler had borrowed.

'Thanks.' I hung up and turned to Randall who was standing beside my shoulder. 'You hear that?'

He nodded. 'Get me copy number two.'

'It was borrowed on Tuesday,' I reminded him, 'by a Miss Carolyn Seaver.'

'The day after you got it back from Cuyler?'

'Right.'

'What's Carolyn Seaver's address? Do you know?'

'Prestonia Towers. On Clark Terrace.'

'Let's go,' said Randall.

★ ★ ★

Our luck was out. So was Miss Seaver. She had left for a visit with friends at the shore, and had taken *The Henchman* with her to read on the plane. The woman in the adjoining apartment gave us this information, but was unable to give us the name, address, or telephone number of the friends Miss Seaver was visiting. 'She'll be home Saturday afternoon — tomorrow,' the neighbor said. 'Can't you wait twenty-four hours? What's so important about a library book?'

Randall was honest with her. 'We don't know ourselves. But it may turn out to be evidence in a crime. Will you ask Miss Seaver to get in touch with me the minute she returns?'

The neighbor's eyes grew round. 'Of course.' Randall gave her his phone number. We thanked her, left, and went back to Cuyler's place where I'd parked my car.

As I climbed out of the police cruiser, Randall said, 'Is *The Henchman* a popular book, Hal?'

15

Randall doesn't know a bestseller from the *Encyclopedia Britannica*. I said, 'Not any more, Lieutenant. The copy we have here hasn't been borrowed for three months, as you can see from the last stamped date on the card envelope. And copy number two — borrowed, it seems, by both Mr. Cuyler and Miss Seaver in less than a month — represents a real burst of business, I should imagine.'

'Have you read it?'

'*The Henchman*?' I shook my head. 'Historical fiction isn't my dish.'

Randall pondered. 'Listen. When you get back to the library, brief your librarians for me, will you?'

'On what?'

'Tell them to inform you — or me — immediately if anyone comes into the library and asks for *The Henchman*. And tell them to find out who's asking, if possible.'

'O.K. And what about the book? Tell anyone who asks that we don't have it?'

'Yeah. Until we check them out. And, Hal — '

'What?'

'Do one more thing for me. *Read* the goddamn book. Maybe something will jump out at you that seems significant.'

'How am I supposed to recognize anything, even if it's there?'

Randall's yellow eyes took on that bland amused look. 'How the hell should I know? *You're* the book detective, aren't you?'

★ ★ ★

The next day — Saturday — I stayed in the library all day, lining up my call sheets for the following week, so I was in my office when Ellen phoned me from her desk. 'Hal?' she said. 'Somebody just asked Joan for your book.

I snapped to attention. '*The Henchman*, you mean?'

'Yes. Joan gave her a song and dance and put her in the reading room.'

'What song and dance?'

'Joan told her we have *The Henchman* but it's out for repair at the bindery. I'm supposed to be checking now on when it'll be back on the shelves.'

'Good for Joan,' I said, 'and good for

you. I'm on my way.' Then, in belated surprise, 'Did you say *her*, Ellen? Is it a woman?'

Ellen whistled lewdly under her breath. 'Wait'll you see her!' she said and hung up.

She was a woman, all right. A blonde, beautiful young woman sitting with her hands clasped around her handbag in one of the reading-room chairs. I went over to her and said, 'The librarian tells me you want to borrow *The Henchman*. It will be back in circulation in just a day or two. If you care to leave your name and telephone number, we'll be glad to call you when the book's available.'

She stood up, and I could see what Ellen's whistle meant. Her figure, which a modish pantsuit did little to hide, was nothing short of spectacular. Every eye in the reading room, male and female, turned her way as though magnetized.

Her face took on a look of disappointment. 'I didn't want to *borrow* the book,' she said. 'I just wanted to look something up in it here in the library. I'm from out of town.'

She didn't look capable of breaking a man's ribs and beating him to death, but maybe she had a friend who was. I said, 'In that case, perhaps we can help you after all. What did you want to look up in *The Henchman?*'

'That's the trouble,' she said. 'I don't really know.'

That shook me a little. I said, 'I've read *The Henchman* myself quite recently, Miss — '

'Elmore,' she said. 'Nancy Elmore.'

'Miss Elmore, maybe if you cared to be a little more specific, I might be able to help you. I'm Hal Johnson. I'm on the library staff.'

Miss Elmore looked around self-consciously. 'Can we go somewhere and talk, Mr. Johnson? I'm sure we're disturbing the people here.'

I didn't think the people in the reading room minded being disturbed by this Miss America candidate, but I said, 'Good idea. I'll just tell the librarian, and we can talk in my office, O.K.?'

Joan, the librarian, was hovering out-side the door of the reading room, her curiosity showing. I told her in a library whisper to call Lieutenant Randall at police headquarters, and tell him that somebody named Nancy Elmore had asked for *The Henchman* and I was about to interview her in my office.

Joan nodded and scurried off.

I had barely got Miss Elmore settled in the one chair in my tiny office when my phone rang. It was Randall. 'Is the girl still there?' he asked.

'Yes.'

'She says her name's Nancy Elmore?'

'Right.'

'Ask her where she's from.'

'What?'

'Are you deaf? Ask her where she's from.'

'Why?'

'Because if she says Minneapolis, she's probably Jefferson Cuyler's niece. The one we notified of his death. Only living relative, remember?'

'Oh.' I looked across my desk at Miss Elmore with new interest.

'Don't let her get away,' Randall said. 'I'll be right over.'

I hung up and turned to Miss Elmore. 'You said you were from out of town, Miss Elmore. Where do you live?'

'Minneapolis. Why?'

I said, 'Nancy Elmore. Minneapolis. I *thought* that name sounded familiar. You've got to be the niece of the man who was killed here yesterday, Jefferson Cuyler. Right?'

She was surprised. 'Yes, that *is* right. I flew in this morning to arrange for Uncle Jeff's funeral as soon as the police release . . . his body.' She swallowed. 'How did you know?'

'I collected some overdue books from your uncle on Monday, Miss Elmore, and he mentioned your name,' I lied. 'That's where I heard it before. Your uncle seemed very proud of you.' *As who wouldn't be?* I was tempted to add.

'Was *The Henchman* one of the books you collected from Uncle Jeff?' she asked. Beautiful, I thought, but definitely not dumb.

'Yes, it was,' I answered carefully, 'so I'm naturally curious to know why you're so interested in it now.'

She gave me an uncertain smile. 'You

won't believe this,' she said. 'It's crazy. Really wild. But Uncle Jeff told me that if he died unexpectedly, I'd find something in that book he wanted me to have.'

'Do you know what it is?'

'I guess it's a kind of a will or legacy or something. But I don't know.'

'When did your uncle tell you this?'

'In a letter I got from him this past Tuesday.'

'Do you have the letter with you?'

She made a new grip on her handbag, which was answer enough. 'As I say, I thought it was crazy — until I was notified yesterday that Uncle Jeff had been killed. Then I thought I'd better do what he said. So, after I checked in at my hotel, I came straight here to the library to look for the book.' Impatience or some other emotion roughened her smooth voice. 'And now it's not even here! So what do I do now?'

'In your place, I'd tell the police about your letter,' I began, just as Lieutenant Randall walked into the room. 'Speak of the devil,' I said. 'Miss Elmore from Minneapolis, this is Lieutenant Randall of our very efficient police department. He's in charge of investigating your uncle's death.'

Randall put his sleepy-looking, unblinking yellow eyes on her. 'If she's really Nancy Elmore from Minneapolis,' he said ungraciously. Then, to her: 'Are you?'

Her answering smile took all of the official starch out of Randall. He appreciates a good-looking woman as well as the next man. 'I'm sorry,' he apologized gruffly, 'but I have to be sure, you know.' He checked the driving license and credit cards she handed him. Then, satisfied, he said to me, 'What about the letter, Hal?'

I told him, making it short.

'Do you mind showing the letter to us, Miss Elmore?' he asked her, as bland as coffee cream now.

She dug in her handbag and came up with it. I read it over Randall's shoulder:

Monday

Dear Nancy,
This is to tell you that the fishing trip of which I wrote you in my last letter went off very well. You'll be glad to

hear that my ailing heart performed splendidly throughout.

I must tell you, however, that upon returning home this morning, I have noted certain disquieting signs that my spell of good fortune may be nearing an end. I won't go into detail but I'll be frank with you: I feel I may suffer an attack at any time now. An attack which might even prove fatal.

I don't want to frighten you, Nancy. But I do want you to be aware that you are my sole heir. Hence this hasty letter, just in case.

You see, my dear, there are reasons, which I won't go into, why I can't just draw up a will in the usual way. So if anything happens to me, I suggest that you visit the main branch of our local public library and ask for a book written by Eugene Stott called The Henchman. In it, you will find my legacy to you, for what it's worth. It will puzzle you, I'm afraid. So I further suggest that you consult our local police about it, showing them this letter. I am confident they will help you locate my estate, and will *see to it, I trust, that you get what is coming to you.*

Affectionately, as always, Uncle Jeff

Randall didn't say anything for a few seconds after he finished reading. Instead, he looked at me and raised his eyebrows.

I nodded. 'I think she ought to know the score,' I said.

Randall gave her the story: the attempted robbery, the murder, the memo-pad writing, the whole thing. Including where copy number two of *The Henchman* was at the moment.

She listened quietly. At the end of his recital, she sighed. 'Poor Uncle Jeff. I honestly thought he might be turning senile when I read that letter. But he wasn't, was he? The 'disquieting signs' in his letter was the attempted robbery. And the 'attack' he feared wasn't a heart attack, but an attack on him by the people who killed him. Do you think he knew who they were?'

'Yes.'

'Then why didn't he tell the police?'

'I don't know,' said Randall, brooding. He tapped the letter with a forefinger.

I put my oar in, just to avoid being forgotten. 'So what do we do now? Wait till Miss Seaver gets home from the shore with *The Henchman*?'

'No.' Randall was emphatic. 'You two are interested primarily in what's in the book. I'm interested in catching a murderer. So we put copy number one of *The Henchman* back on the shelves, Hal. And its file index card back in the cabinet. And we hope very hard that the murderer will still come in today and try to get the book.' He reached for my phone. 'I'll put a man in the library to nab anybody else who shows interest in it.'

★   ★   ★

When I got back, Randall and Nancy Elmore were leaving. 'When we hear from Miss Seaver,' Randall was saying to her, 'I'll be in touch.'

She thanked him, and gave him the name of her hotel. He said he'd drop her off there on his way back to Headquarters. Then she thanked me too, and they left.

'Jimmy Coogan is on his way over to babysit the book,' Randall said over his shoulder. 'Will you watch it until he gets here?'

'Sure,' I said.

I went to the reading room and took a seat to the right of the double-door entrance. From there, I could see the shelf where I'd put *The Henchman*, could even make out the crimson cover of the book itself.

It was just as well I took up my vigil when I did, because it wasn't five minutes after Randall left that the action started.

A massive chunky man with shaggy hair and a drooping mustache hove into view at the far end of the aisle of bookshelves I was watching. He had the muscular, sure-footed look of a pro fullback. His big shoulders strained the seams of the windbreaker he wore. As he came towards me, I caught a brief glimpse of his face: blunt features, small eyes sunk in deep sockets, a thin slash of a mouth under the mustache. Unlike the beautiful Miss Elmore, I thought, this specimen would be capable of breaking a man's ribs and beating him to death. He carried a battered black briefcase in one hand.

He moved unhurriedly up the aisle of bookshelves, his eyes turning from side to side as he scanned the numbers on the spines of the books, obviously seeking a certain number and a certain book.

It was warm in the reading room, but cold fingers touched my spine.

I got the tight feeling in my stomach I used to get at the start of action when I was a real cop. After my relatively peaceful time as a library detective, the old sensation, oddly enough, was almost pleasant, a reminder of more exciting times. From behind a copy of *Newsweek*, I watched the man.

Suddenly he halted, reached out a hand, and plucked a book from the shelf. The book with the crimson cover. *The Henchman*. At the same time he gave a nod of satisfaction, as though congratulating himself on a stroke of good luck.

He raised his eyes to look around him. I dropped mine to the magazine. Evidently he saw nothing to alarm him, because when I risked a surreptitious look he was in the act of opening the book.

While I watched, he gave the book a superficial examination: first leafing rapidly through it, then holding it upside down by its covers and shaking it to dislodge anything that might be lying loose between its pages. Finding nothing, he pried up with his fingernail one corner of the card envelope in the front of the book and peered beneath it. Again nothing. He paused, considering his next move.

I was fairly sure what that move would be — a more thorough inspection of the book in a more private place. And I was right. After another quick survey of his surroundings, he casually opened his briefcase, put *The Henchman* in it, and turned to leave.

I stood up and followed him toward Ellen's check-out desk, knowing with absolute certainty that he didn't intend to stop for Ellen to check out the book in the usual way. Ellen, busy with a half dozen customers, didn't even look up as he strode past her desk.

I caught up with him in the lobby before he was able to push through the glass doors of the exit. I tapped him on the shoulder from behind.

For the space of half a breath, he kept going. Then he halted and swung around, his eyes mean. 'What?'

'You've forgotten something, haven't you, sir?' I asked in my smoothest library voice.

'Forgot what?' His knuckles tightened on the handle of the briefcase.

'I believe you forgot to check out the library book in your briefcase.'

He blinked. 'Who the hell are you?'

'A member of the library staff. I must ask you to check out your book in the usual way before removing it from the library.'

'I don't have any book of yours, buster. Get lost.' He began to turn away.

'I saw you put it in your briefcase,' I said. I was beginning to sweat. What was I thinking of, bracing him before Jimmy Coogan arrived to back me up? For I knew after tapping that iron-solid shoulder that I couldn't take this gorilla alone the best day I ever lived.

He gave me a tight grin, displaying yellow teeth with a gap between the upper fronts. 'You got it all wrong,' he said. 'I'll tell you one more time. I don't *have* a book of yours. So drop dead.'

'Let's just have a look in your briefcase,' I suggested mildly. 'That ought to settle it.'

'Not a chance, pal. This briefcase is private property. *My* private property. That means it ain't open to the public. So goodbye.' He turned his back and started for the exit doors again.

I let him go, deciding with a feeling of immense relief that discretion in this case seemed the better part of you-know-what. That is, I let him go until I caught a glimpse of the cheerful Irish countenance of Jimmy Coogan climbing the library steps. It was a heartening sight: so heartening that I grabbed the book thief by one arm — the arm with the briefcase — and whirled him around again. I said sternly, 'I can arrest you, you know. So why not cooperate?'

'*Arrest* me?' He laughed out loud. 'You

and who else, Junior?'

'Me and Detective Coogan of the Police Department,' I said with a touch of smugness, 'who is now coming through the door behind you.' I raised my voice. 'Hey, Jimmy! Here's a customer for you.'

The man snarled like an animal and swung around, poised for flight. Coogan blocked his way. 'Hold it!' he advised in a quiet tone that snapped like a whip. 'What's going on here?'

'This guy's stealing one of our books,' I said, giving Coogan a meaningful look. 'It's in his briefcase.'

'Is that so, now?' Coogan murmured. 'Would you mind opening the case, sir?'

'Why should I? There's no book in it.'

'Yes, there is,' I insisted. 'A book called *The Henchman*.' Another meaningful glance at Coogan.

Coogan clicked his tongue reprovingly. 'In that case, sir,' he said cheerfully, 'I'm afraid you'll have to come downtown with me until we straighten this out. I'll just take charge of your briefcase in the meantime.' He held out his hand, giving his prisoner a flash of his ID.

I could almost see the wheels going around in the thief's head. *This is no big deal*, he was telling himself. *At the most, they've got me for book theft — a crummy misdemeanor that I can settle by returning the book or paying for it.*

After a moment's hesitation, he nodded sullenly, and handed the briefcase to Coogan. I said, 'Get him out of here, Jimmy, O.K.? Before we upset the whole library. I'm glad you showed up when you did.' I winked at Coogan. 'I don't think I could have handled him alone.'

Coogan beamed at the thief. 'But you won't give me any trouble, will you now?' he asked politely. Coogan can afford to be polite. He stands six feet five and weighs in at two-sixty on the police scales.

★　★　★

At four o'clock, Randall called me. 'Thanks for Slenski,' he said.

'Slenski? Is that his name?'

'Yeah. Truck driver based in Detroit. He could be our man, Hal. Although he denies it, of course.'

'Both the break-in and the murder?'

'We've already checked him out in Detroit. The trucking outfit he works for says his schedule put him here in town both last weekend and this.'

'But he has airtight alibis for both nights, no doubt.'

'Certainly.' There was a shrug in Randall's voice. 'When he's in town, he always stays with a waitress at the Radio Bar, name of Ellie Slack. And Ellie Slack tells us that Slenski was with her both of the nights in question. All night.'

'Lying through her teeth?'

'Probably. Slenski also claims she recommended *The Henchman* to him as a good yarn to kill time with between runs.'

I said, 'That ought to prove she's a liar. Even a bar waitress would know it's no kind of book for a truck driver.'

'Slenski says he thought he'd just 'borrow' it from the public library and return it the next time he hits town — less trouble than all the red tape of applying for a non-resident library card, and so forth. Obviously a crock. But we can't prove he's lying. At least, not yet.'

'He's lying,' I said. 'Take my word for it.'

Randall laughed. He seemed in high good humor. 'He's offered to pay for your damned book, so don't badmouth him.'

'Well, that's generous. You're holding him all the same, aren't you?'

'Sure. At least until we find out what's in Miss Seaver's copy of *The Henchman*. I'm hoping that'll point us toward some sort of a connection between Slenski and Cuyler. So far, we can't find any.'

'How about Miss Seaver?' I said. 'Is she home yet?'

'That's why I called. She's home. Are you free to go with us to pick up the book?'

'I wouldn't miss it for the world,' I said.

'We'll meet you at the library's main entrance in twenty minutes.'

★　★　★

Miss Seaver didn't mind in the least giving up her copy of *The Henchman*. 'I didn't even finish it,' she said. 'It's a poorly written, predictable story, and I can't imagine how it could possibly be connected with a crime . . . '

Randall suggested that she watch the newspapers to see if it actually *was* connected with a crime, and we left.

The lieutenant pretended to be calm and properly official about the book, but he was just as anxious to learn its secret, if any, as Miss Elmore and me. Or else Miss Elmore's Christmas-morning look of anticipation won him over. He handed me the volume as we settled into the police car for the ride back to town, and said, 'Here, Hal, you're the book expert. Give it a look while I drive.'

I obliged. And of course, once you knew there was something to find in the book, finding it proved to be easy. What we were looking for wasn't in the book at all, as it turned out; it was *behind* the book. When I bent the covers back on themselves, held the book up against the light and peered through the opening between the spine and the binding, I could see it plainly. 'There's *something* here, Lieutenant,' I said, keeping my voice level for Miss Elmore's benefit, although I felt excitement quickening my pulse.

Randall took his eyes off the road briefly. 'What is it?'

'It looks like a key,' I said. I shook the book hard. 'It's glued, I guess — to the inner surface of the spine.'

'Well, get it out,' Randall directed.

Easier said than done. The key must have been cemented to the inside of the spine cover with epoxy or something of the sort, because it stubbornly refused to be pried loose. In the end, I cut the book cover through with my pocket knife, and jimmied the key loose with the screwdriver from the toolkit of the police car.

When I had the key free, Lieutenant Randall pulled over to the curb and parked, leaving the motor running. 'Let's see it,' he said.

I handed the key to him. Flat, about two inches long, with a rounded head, it looked something like a standard safe-deposit-box key; yet the notches cut into only one edge of the flat shank were far too simple and uncomplicated for that. The number 97 was stamped into the head.

Randall grinned at Miss Elmore. 'Well, here's your legacy,' he said.

'What do you suppose it's a key to?'

Randall turned the key in his fingers. 'A locker of some sort, I'd guess.'

I thought he was right. 'Bus station, maybe?' I suggested.

He shrugged. 'Could be. Or bowling alley, country club, railroad station, city club, almost anywhere. So all we'll have to do is try the key on number 97 of every bank of lockers in the city.'

I didn't say anything because I knew he wasn't serious. Miss Elmore said, 'But I know poor Uncle Jeff didn't belong to any kind of club, so that should narrow it down, shouldn't it?'

'How about the YMCA?' Randall asked.

'Yes!' Miss Elmore cried. 'He *did* belong to the YMCA! He went swimming twice a week in the YMCA pool. How did you guess that?'

'Just routine police work,' Randall answered, deadpan. Then, 'Look under the cement.' He handed her the key.

Peering over her shoulder, breathing

her carnation scent, I could see too, through the hardened gob of transparent cement still adhering to the key head, four small letters stamped into the metal: YMCA.

When Randall and I went into the locker room of the YMCA fifteen minutes later, Miss Elmore remained in the police car outside. All she said as we left her was, 'Please hurry! I'm dying of curiosity!'

The locker room was sparsely populated: maybe a dozen men, mostly young, dressing or undressing, none of them in the aisle of lockers we wanted. We stopped in front of locker 97 and had our first surprise.

Locker 97 wasn't locked. What was more, there wasn't even a keyhole in the door to show that it *could* be locked. 'Ouch!' I murmured.

Randall swore under his breath, grabbed the door handle, tripped the latch, and pulled the locker door open wide.

We breathed easier. The lower left segment inside was a locker within a locker — a little built-in safe in which you could leave your valuables, I guess, while you were swimming, playing basketball, or working out in the gym. The inner locker was locked. It had a keyhole. And Uncle Jeff's key slid into it smooth as grease.

Randall took a breath, raised his eyebrows at me, turned the key, and opened up.

We found ourselves looking at three bulging canvas bags crammed together into the three cubic feet of locker space. The bags had the words 'Crane Security Express' stenciled on them. And they contained, as Randall told me later, three hundred and eleven thousand dollars in cash.

★ ★ ★

A few days later, over a pizza and beer which he insisted on paying for, Randall told me the rest of the story. I suppose it was his way of thanking me for my help in what he was already calling The Henchman Case.

'Cuyler was working for Crane Security

when he had his heart attack and had to retire a year or so ago. But he only had his Social Security payments to live on because he hadn't been with Crane long enough to qualify for a pension. So there he was, a widower, a semi-invalid with an uncertain future, and all alone in the world except for a niece in Minneapolis.'

'Yum,' I said.

'Shut up, Hal,' he said. 'Do you want to hear this or don't you?'

'Continue,' I urged him, 'please.'

'Cuyler is bitter at his rotten luck in being so poor so suddenly. He decides he'll try to steal enough money from his old firm to live high on the hog for whatever time he has left. After all, they wouldn't even pay him a pension, the ungrateful tightwads.'

I said, 'Where does your truck driver come in?'

'Cuyler hired him to do the actual robbery. He hadn't the nerve to do it himself.'

'I remember the heist,' I said. 'A Crane Security Express van, loaded with cash for three or four payroll deliveries, was cleaned out in the parking lot of some diner while the guards were having lunch inside.'

'Slenski did the cleaning-out. Cuyler waited around the corner in the getaway car. It was a cozy set-up. Cuyler knew all about the routes, schedules, pick-ups, and deliveries of the Crane vans; he also knew the guards on that particular van always stopped for lunch on Fridays at that diner and left the van unattended in the parking lot. He managed to get keys to the van's door-locks, too.'

Something was bothering me. I said, 'Two questions, Lieutenant. You told me we recovered the entire loot from the van robbery in Cuyler's YMCA locker. So why hadn't Cuyler spent any of it since the robbery? And what did the truck driver get out of the caper?'

Randall said, 'Cuyler was probably waiting for the heat to die down a bit before he began spending hot money. As for Slenski's cut, it was five thousand dollars — a good chunk of Cuyler's savings — paid to Slenski half before-hand, and the other half when Slenski turned over the loot to Cuyler. Slenski went off home to Detroit, apparently pleased with his windfall. But he didn't stay pleased very long. When he had a chance to think things over, he realized he'd been taken. And he decided not to hold still for it.'

'So he tried to help himself to a bigger cut when he broke into Cuyler's house that Sunday night?' I said.

'Sure. Who else would make such a shambles of the place?'

'So Cuyler figures he'll try again. Maybe right away. And telling the cops is out for obvious reasons. Even though he suspects Slenski may cut up pretty rough on his next visit.'

'That's when he decided to write that letter to his niece, and to hide the key to his YMCA locker in your library book. He wanted his niece to know the score if anything happened to him.'

'It seems to me it would have been simpler all around to send the key to his niece in the letter.'

'It would. But Cuyler definitely intended to enjoy that money himself if he had the chance. And he was afraid, maybe, that his niece would get so curious about the key that she might find out he was a thief while he was still alive. And he didn't want that.'

I finished off my pizza and drained my beer mug. I said, 'Come on, Lieutenant, you used to lecture me about the rules of evidence. What evidence — *hard* evidence — do you have that Slenski actually beat up Cuyler and caused his death? As far as you know and can prove, Slenski is just a petty out-of-town thief who snitched a book from our public library here. Isn't that right?'

'No, it isn't right.' There was honey in Randall's voice. 'Didn't I tell you, Hal? We found a memo in Slenski's wallet the day you turned him in. Oddly enough, the memo said: '*The Henchman* Eugene Stott Public Library,' and was in the very same handwriting as *our* memo from Cuyler's house. We knew we had him cold for Cuyler's killing before we found the Crane Security Express loot.'

'Mercy,' I said, 'you do play them close to your vest, don't you, Lieutenant?'

'When we showed him we had him all wrapped up for murder, he sang like a canary to get his rap reduced. How do you think we learned all this jazz about the robbery?'

'Routine police work,' I said, grinning. I was quiet for a minute, thinking. Then I said, 'The real screwball in the whole mess was handsome Uncle Jeff, if you ask me.'

'I'm not asking you. But why?'

'That nutty letter to his niece, for one thing. Telling her he was leaving her a legacy in a library book, then telling her to go to the *police*, for God's sake, to be sure she got it. That was a great legacy to go to the police about! Three hundred thousand *stolen* dollars!'

Randall laughed. 'Old Cuyler wasn't so dumb, Hal.'

'No?'

'No. You're forgetting the reward.'

I was. It had been widely advertised at the time of the robbery. Twenty-five thousand to anybody supplying information leading to the arrest of the thieves or the recovery of the money. I said, 'You mean Nancy Elmore gets the reward?'

'Sure,' said Randall. 'The least I could do was to see she collected it.' He paused. 'Of course, Miss Elmore did see fit to write a big fat check for the Police Widows and Orphans Fund before she left for Minneapolis.'

'How peachy for the Widows and Orphans,' I said. 'But *I* found the key in the book, remember. *I* snagged the murderer for you. Don't I get something for that?'

'Sorry,' said Randall, his cat's eyes showing amusement, 'but you're neither a widow nor an orphan, Hal. Will you settle for another beer?'

'I guess I'll have to,' I said sadly.

2

The Young Runners

It was the worst kind of tenement. In the 1200 block of Gardenia Street, I checked my list to be sure I had the address right. Then I went inside, looking for a young man named Jasper Jones.

In my capacity as a library cop, I'd been in the neighborhood before, trying to trace books that had been stolen from the public library. This time, however, I was on Gardenia Street merely to collect an overdue book. A routine call.

Gardenia Street. The littered filthy hallway of the tenement didn't smell like gardenias, believe me. Luckily, the room I was looking for was on the ground floor. I rapped lightly on the door.

It was cautiously opened a few inches by a once-pretty woman with a pale face and a do-it-yourself blonde dye job. She peered out at me with tired-looking eyes.

'Yes?'

'I'm looking for Jasper Jones,' I said. 'Is he here?'

Sudden concern made her tired eyes even more tired. 'Jasper? He's not home from school yet. What's he done?' she asked. 'Has Jasper done something? Who are you?'

I told her, and showed her my ID card from the library.

'Oh,' she said, relieved. 'Well, Jasper isn't home yet, like I said. I'm sorry.'

'You're Mrs. Jones? Jasper's mother?'

'That's right.' She perked up a little, fluffing her hair with one hand. She didn't invite me in, though.

'Maybe you can help me then, Mrs. Jones. If you can find Jasper's overdue library book and pay me the small fine he owes on it, I won't need to bother Jasper at all.'

She said, 'Jasper's really a terrific reader for an eleven-year-old, Mr. Johnson.' There was pride in her voice. 'And, consequently, he gets so many books from the public library that I can't even begin to keep track of them. So . . . '

'He borrows a lot of books, all right,' I agreed. 'Our children's librarian told me that. But this is the first time Jasper's ever failed to return a book on time. So it's no big deal, Mrs. Jones. With his excellent record, I'll even forget the fine if you'll just give me the book.'

'I'm sorry, Mr. Johnson.' Mrs. Jones sounded harried. 'I'm trying to get dressed to go to work, and I'm late, okay? Can't you find Jasper and ask *him* about your book? I haven't got time to look for it right now.'

'Sure,' I said. 'Where'll I find him?'

'Well, you can either wait here till he gets home, or you can probably find him in the park two blocks down. He usually stops there on his way home from school.'

'Thanks, Mrs. Jones.' I left her and went out, and took a deep breath of the polluted outside air. It smelled as fresh as gardenias compared with the air in the tenement hallway.

I walked the two blocks down Gardenia to Mrs. Jones's 'park.' It turned out to be a playground. No trees, flowers, grass, or rustic benches. Just a sun-baked expanse of bare beaten earth, enclosed by a chain-link fence eight feet high. At one end of the enclosure was a mounted basketball hoop, and I could make out the faint markings of old softball bases in the dust. A bunch of kids, some black, some white, of all ages up to about fifteen, was having a high old time in a pickup basketball game beneath the single basket. There was a lot of yelling, jumping, and juvenile cursing, and a lot of wild set and hook shots that never came near the basket. Another bunch of kids was standing around, offering comments and waiting for a chance to get into the game.

It was evident that Jasper Jones wasn't the only ghetto kid to stop here on his way home from school, because textbooks, homework papers, and bulging book bags were scattered on the ground along the inside of the wire fence. Three battered old bicycles, and one that looked almost new, were leaning against the fence too. I went into the playground and walked along the fence past the books and bicycles toward the knot of nonparticipants in the game. They watched me come in unfriendly silence. I didn't know whether their unfriendliness was because I was dressed so well for this neighborhood, or because they smelled cop on me. Probably the latter. I'd been a Homicide cop for quite a few years before I switched to the public library, and I knew that these streetwise ghetto kids could smell fuzz a mile off — even harmless library fuzz like me.

I went up to a tall gangly black boy who had outgrown his windbreaker by six inches and said politely, 'Can you tell me if Jasper Jones is around?'

He treated me to a long thoughtful stare before he replied, 'Who wants to know?' He wasn't being arrogant or nasty, just cautious.

'I'm from the public library and Jasper has an overdue book I want to collect,' I said. 'Is he here?'

'Yeah,' said the boy in the windbreaker, making up his mind. He turned and shouted toward the players, 'Hey, Jazz! Guy to see you!' I could feel the hostility around me subside.

The youngster who responded to this

summons was small for his age. He had a shock of black unruly hair, a thin face with a pointed chin, and two of the brightest blue eyes I've ever seen. The eyes were older than the kid. He said to the tall boy who had called him out of the game, 'Go in for me, will you, George?' I thought Jasper's team would benefit by the change. For tall George was obviously better equipped as a basketball player than this short eleven-year-old that faced me.

He was panting a little from his recent exertions on the basketball court. He led me away from the other kids a few steps and said, 'Yeah? You want me?' His blue eyes looked me over.

'If you're Jasper Jones, I do. I came to get a library book from you, Jasper.'

'Call me Jazz,' he said cockily. 'Everybody does.' Then, 'A library book?' he repeated. 'I never saw you before, did I?'

'Not that I know of. What difference does that make? I still have to collect the library book from you. It's four weeks overdue.' I showed him my library identification card.

'Oh!' he said. In some curious way, his steady blue eyes seemed to be reassessing me. 'Overdue? What's the name of the book, mister? You must be wrong. I never keep a book out too long.'

'We sent you an overdue notice, Jazz. Didn't you get it?'

He looked blank. 'Nope. I suppose Mom didn't bother telling me. Anyway, what's the book?'

I said, '*The Robber of Featherbed Lane*. Remember it?'

He shook his head. 'Naw. I read 'em so fast I don't even bother to look at their names half the time.'

'Well,' I said, letting some of my impatience show, 'I've come all the way out here to get that book, Jazz, so let's go back to your place and find it, huh?'

Jasper looked over my shoulder into the distance. 'No use going to my place,' he said uncomfortably. 'It's not there.'

'How do you know till you look?'

'I just know, that's all, man.' He raised his eyes to mine.

'That's no answer. How do you know?'

He frowned in thought. At length, he

said, 'I guess I'll have to tell you.' His expression was half hangdog belligerent, half proud. 'I've got this little business going on the side with your library books, man, and that particular book — '

I interrupted him. 'A little business on the side? What kind of business? Are you *selling* our library books?'

He was scornful. 'You're not too sharp, are you, mister? If I was selling your crummy books, how come none of 'em ever turned up missing before?'

He had me there. 'So what is this business of yours?' I asked.

'I don't sell your books, I rent them,' explained Jasper Jones blandly.

I couldn't keep from grinning at him. A rental library operated by an eleven-year-old businessman with somebody else's books was something I'd never run into before. I said as severely as I could, 'You mean you rent all those books you get from the public library to other kids?'

'Sure.' Unrepentant. 'After I've read 'em myself, why not?'

'Can't they apply for library cards and borrow their own books — for free?'

'I save 'em a lot of time and trouble by letting 'em read mine. They pay me a nickel apiece and promise to put 'em in the library book-drop before the date on the card. And that saves *me* a lot of trouble. I don't have to keep track of the dates and return 'em myself.'

'Some racket,' I said. 'Do you make much money at it?'

He beamed. 'I made enough the last coupla years to buy me that set of wheels over there.' He pointed proudly at the almost-new bicycle leaning against the fence. There was a big book bag on the flat luggage rack above the rear wheel. Jasper, suddenly cautious, asked anxiously. 'It's okay for me to do that, isn't it? Rent library books, I mean? Long as the books are back on time?'

I laughed. 'As far as I know, there's no law against lending — or renting — public library books to other people besides the cardholder. Always providing, of course, the library gets its books back in good shape.' I fixed him with a stern look. 'Which brings us back to *The Robber of Featherbed Lane*. Do you

55

know which of your — ah — customers you rented that one to?'

'Yeah.' He hesitated. 'Solly Joseph. That's why I didn't tell you. Solly's in the class behind me at school. And Solly's old man got drunk and tore your library book all to pieces because he didn't want Solly reading anything about robbers, see?' Jasper sighed heavily. 'So I guess I got to pay for the book, right?'

'Right,' I said. 'Or your mother or father or somebody.'

He said, 'I'll pay for it myself. Mom never has any bread. She's only working part-time. And my old man went off somewhere a coupla years ago.'

'Okay,' I said. 'Three-fifty. Kids' books run kind of high these days. I'm sorry.'

'Forget it,' he said with a chopping gesture. 'I'll collect it from Solly, don't worry.' He took an old-fashioned coin purse from his jeans, opened it, and counted out $3.50 into my hand — two one-dollar bills and the rest in small change. 'Is that it?'

'That's it.' I grinned at him. He was quite a kid. 'Now, you better get back in that basketball game, Jazz. Your friend George just missed an easy layup.'

Everybody at the library got a big kick out of my story about Jasper Jones and his book-rental operation. And about Solly Joseph's old man getting drunk and destroying one of our children's books because it might have a bad influence on Solly. Olive Gaston, head children's librarian, was especially amused. 'That little Jasper Jones goes out of here every Saturday morning as regular as clockwork,' she said, 'with so many books in his book-bag he can hardly carry it. So *that's* why he takes so many. He rents them. He always tells me it's because he's such a fast reader.'

I turned in the kid's $3.50 along with the day's fines, and forgot about Jasper Jones until several weeks later when Lieutenant Randall, my former boss at the police department, brought the incident back to mind.

We were having a pizza and beer together in Tony's Diner, having met there at Randall's suggestion. He made it clear, however, that I was not his guest; I could pay for my own pizza out of the princely salary the library paid me for being what he called a 'sissy' cop. Randall has never forgiven me for leaving him and the Department and seeking a more literate — not to mention, more literary — association.

I started on my pizza and opened with my usual query. 'Well, how many murders did you solve today, Lieutenant?'

Normally he'll answer this with a sour glance from his spooky eyes and a contemptuous belch if he's drinking beer. Tonight, however, he replied promptly, as though on cue. 'One,' he said.

'One?' I raised my eyebrows. 'A new record. Congratulations.'

'Don't knock it,' he said. 'It lets me do you a little favor.'

'A favor?' I stared at him. 'You feeling all right?'

'I feel fine,' he said, chomping on a large section of pizza to prove it.

'Then for God's sake tell me about it.'

He shrugged, obviously pleased that I'd given him the lead. 'Nothing much to it,' he apologized. 'Routine stuff. Fellow got stabbed in a bar in a quarrel with a former girlfriend about his present girlfriend. He made it home and quietly bled to death. You remember that kind, don't you? From when you were a real cop?' He underlined the word *real* with his voice.

'Yeah,' I said, 'I remember.' And I did. It made me a little homesick for Homicide, but not much.

'When they discovered the stiff about midnight,' Randall went on, 'they called me and I went out there. Ghetto room on South Wildflower.'

'And you solved the case instantly?'

'Took about half an hour. Three witnesses in the bar saw the stabbing and could identify the stabber. We've got the murderess sewed up tight.'

'Where does a favor for me come into it?' It's hard for me to tell, even after all these years, when Lieutenant Randall is kidding and when he's serious.

'That's the real reason I called you tonight, Hal. Kind of a curious thing, but I saw right away last night that I could do you some good.'

'You going to tell me how?'

'Certainly. But answer a question first. You probably think of me as a tough, unappreciative, demanding type who asks for favors but never returns one, right?' Randall's unwinking cat's eyes gleamed in the fluorescent lights of the diner.

'Right,' I agreed heartily, playing along.

'So I go out to where this fellow bleeds to death and look over the scene, and to my utter amazement,' said Randall, grinning like a chimpanzee with a banana in view, 'I discover something that makes me think of you immediately.'

'What? Either tell me or shut up.'

He took a long swallow of beer. 'You wouldn't have dared talk to me that way in the old days,' he complained.

'That's one reason I left you.'

He wiped beer foam off his lips with a paper napkin. Then he said with dignity, 'You've done me several favors since you left the department, Hal. I'll admit it. You've helped me solve a couple of my major cases. So now I'm going to help you solve one of *your* major cases. Tit for tat. And prove that I'm not as unappreciative as you think.'

'Hurry up,' I said, 'before I start to cry or sing 'Hearts and Flowers.' '

He grinned. 'What I'm going to do for you, pal, is to save you a lot of time and trouble — and an unnecessary trip to South 1 Wildflower Street.'

I sat up. Despite himself, Lieutenant Randall was beginning to interest me. 'Yeah?' I said.

'Yeah.' He was enjoying himself.

'How come?'

'Well, when I got out there and the M.E. had taken a gander at the stiff, I kind of cased the dead guy's room a little bit.' Randall made a face. 'It was a dump. Filth, stench, a real pigsty, you know?'

I nodded. I remembered that from my cop days, too.

'But the surprise was, I found a book under the guy's bed,' said Randall, smirking. 'The only book in the whole joint. Like he'd thrown it under the bed and forgotten about it. And you know what it was?'

'A library book?' I guessed.

'Right. And I looked at the card in it, and you know something? That book was way overdue, Hal. Think of that! Over-due! That's a pretty heinous crime in library circles, I said to myself. So what did I generously decide to do? I decided to bring the book in for you, thus saving you the arduous job of tracking the damn thing down and bringing your criminal to justice!' He leaned back and made an expansive gesture.

I said, 'You're all heart, Lieutenant. Where's the book?'

'I've got it. Don't fret yourself, son. But there's a couple of funny things about it that probably call for the attention of an expert book detective like yourself.'

'Such as?'

'Such as the fact that it says inside the front cover of the book that it's intended for kids from ten to fourteen years old. And this murdered man of mine was twenty-seven if he was a day.' Randall snickered into his beer glass.

'A kid's book? Well — ' I paused. 'Maybe your murder victim was what we call a reluctant reader. There's no disgrace in reading kids' books, you know, even if you're grown up.'

'I understand that. And you think he may have been one of your reluctant-reader types, is that it?'

'Maybe.'

He shook his head solemnly. 'No way, Hal. This guy was a cheap hood with a record as long as your arm. The only reading he ever did was the sports page and the racing form. And what's more, he was a junkie. Hooked like a mackerel, judging from all the mainline needle marks on him. So what's with the children's literature under the bed?'

I shrugged. 'Beats me.'

'No solutions from the famous book detective, Hal Johnson?'

'Not tonight,' I said. 'Now you've pulled your gag, let's have the book.'

Right then was when I suddenly recalled my eleven-year-old friend Jasper Jones. For the book Randall handed to me over the table was *The Robber of Featherbed Lane*. I looked at him. 'Was the name of your stabbing victim Joseph, by any chance?'

'Yeah. How'd you guess that? Although he was better known as Joe.'

I relaxed a little. 'Joe what?'
'Joe Sabatini,' Randall said.

★ ★ ★

More out of curiosity than anything else, I checked the book against our records the next day to see if it could possibly be the copy that Jasper Jones had reported destroyed by Solly Joseph's drunken father. With four or five copies of most juvenile books circulating through our library system, it was unlikely this could be Jasper Jones's overdue book.

But it was.

My first thought was that Solly Joseph had told Jasper Jones a big lie about what happened to the book he'd rented. My second thought was that, if so, Jasper had probably taken $3.50 out of Solly's hide by this time. My third thought was that I ought to return Jasper's money now that our book was recovered. My fourth thought was that the fines on the book almost equaled $3.50 by now, anyway, so why bother? And my fifth thought was, belatedly enough, that maybe Jasper Jones was the one who'd been lying.

I stopped counting at that point and just let my memory of Jasper's conversation with me slosh around in my head. Right away several curious angles occurred to me that I hadn't noticed at the time. For one thing, I now found it rather puzzling that when I'd told Jasper I'd come to collect a library book from him, his initial reaction was to ask me a strange question: 'I never saw you before, did I?' Then, when I'd explained it was an *overdue* library book and identified myself, his whole manner had undergone a subtle change. And while claiming not to remember *The Robber of Featherbed Lane* at first, he'd later remembered exactly what had been done to that particular book by Solly Joseph's intoxicated father.

I didn't want to believe that an eleven-year-old ghetto kid had been able to con an old pro like me so easily. But the conviction grew. During my rounds that day, doubts about Jasper Jones kept flagging at me.

I got back to the library about three in the afternoon, and after sitting in my office for ten minutes, looking at the wall, I reached for the phone and dialed Gardenia Street Grade School. I explained to the secretary in the principal's office who I was, telling her the truth. Then I embroidered it a little. 'A couple of kids from your school have applied for cards at the public library,' I told her, 'and we're checking them out before we issue the cards.' Nonsense, of course, but the secretary didn't know that. 'Would you be good enough to confirm that they're bona-fide students in your school?'

'Certainly,' she said. 'What are their names?'

'Jasper Jones,' I said. 'Probably in the fifth or sixth grade. Maybe seventh. And Solly — or Solomon — Joseph, around fifth grade, I guess.'

She went off to check their rolls and when she came back on she said, 'Jasper Jones is in our sixth grade. But we have no Solly or Solomon Joseph in any grade that I can find. Does that help you?'

'Enormously,' I said. 'I had doubts about Joseph myself and you've confirmed them.' I thanked her and hung up.

So there was no Solly Joseph in the class behind Jasper Jones at Gardenia Street School. How about that? Solly had been made up out of whole cloth for my benefit, apparently. And Solly's drunken father, too.

On my way home that evening I took *The Robber of Featherbed Lane* with me to police headquarters, and without stopping first at Randall's office I paid a visit to my old sidekick, Jerry Baskin, who heads up the police laboratory. I handed him the book and asked him as a personal favor to give it his best going-over, and let me know if he found anything out of the way about it. And not — repeat, *not* — to say anything about it to anyone at the department until I gave him the word.

He agreed, for old times' sake. And for the fifth of J & B Scotch which just happened to be peeking out of my car-coat pocket.

'What am I supposed to be looking for?' Jerry asked me, uncapping the Scotch and taking a luxurious sniff of its rich aroma.

'Anything,' I said. 'Or nothing. I don't

know. But give it your best shot, will you?'

'Okay,' said Jerry. 'I'll call you.'

He called me the following afternoon. 'Your library book, Hal,' he said without preamble. 'I found something.'

'What?' I asked.

'Traces of heroin in the card pocket.'

'Heroin?' My heart gave a sickening lurch. 'You sure?'

'Mexican, I'd guess. Not enough to analyze for quality. But definitely heroin, Hal.'

'I was afraid of that.' I paused, thinking. I wanted to be sure. I said, 'Will you give some other books the same treatment for me, Jerry?'

'Why not?' Jerry said. 'At a bottle of Scotch per book, what can I lose?'

I went to the children's library and took from the shelves half a dozen of the books borrowed by Jasper Jones and recently returned. Olive Gaston dug them up for me without comment, and I took them over to Jerry Baskin. With only one more bottle of J & B, however, not half a dozen. I can't afford to be a spendthrift on my anemic library expense account.

Jerry reported his findings on the additional books two days later: three of the six books I'd given him showed traces of heroin in the card pockets. 'Anything else?' I asked him.

'A shred of glassine paper in one card pocket, Hal.'

That's when I went to see Lieutenant Randall. Facing him across his scarred desk, I said, 'You remember that library book you found under Joe Sabatini's bed?'

'What about it?'

I told him the whole story. Throughout my recital, he didn't move; he didn't blink his cat's eyes once. I finished up by saying morosely, 'I'm sure the kid isn't on smack himself. So all I can come up with is that he's a pusher. That he's not renting library books to his pals, but passing them out to his customers with packets of heroin in the card pockets. What's more innocent-looking than a kid's library book? This is an eleven-year-old kid, Lieutenant! I can't believe it!'

Randall lit a cigarette. 'You've been out of touch too long, Hal. Messing around with your library books. The Narc boys are arresting kids as young as Jasper Jones every day. Didn't you know that?'

'No.'

'They are. And even younger. The kids are recruited to the drug trade primarily because they *are* kids, Hal. Juveniles. If they get caught possessing or selling heroin, they're treated leniently by the courts as juvenile delinquents. But if *adults* get caught doing the same thing, they get a mandatory life sentence under state law. See how it works? The kids run all the risks of handling the dope, while their bosses, the older pushers, just hang around on the edges, picking up the money and dodging that life sentence. They call the kids their 'runners' or 'holders.' And half the time the kids don't even realize what they're doing.'

I remembered Jasper Jones's old-young blue eyes and the facility with which he had improvised the story about Solly Joseph. 'I'm afraid my kid knows what he's doing,' I said.

'Well, they all know they're doing something not quite legal, put it that way.

But they usually don't realize the enormous street value of the stuff they're handling. Most of them work for peanuts, or a new bike, or for kicks, or because somebody they admire — like an older pusher, say — asks them to.'

I could understand how that would happen. The pusher's a big man in the neighborhood. He wears fancy clothes, drives luxury automobiles, is always flashing money. The kids look up to him, want to be like him. They gladly do what he asks. I said, 'So the kids take the heat? And the adult pushers go free?' I felt very depressed.

Randall nodded. 'Usually.'

'Lieutenant,' I said grimly, 'will you do me a favor? A real one this time?'

'Another?' Randall smiled tightly. 'What did you have in mind?'

'I want you to turn my Jasper Jones information over to the Narcotics Squad downstairs for action. But I'd like you to insist on one thing for me to Lieutenant Logan: that they identify and get the goods — possession, peddling, the works — on Jasper's adult pusher before they arrest Jasper Jones.'

Randall said, 'I guess I can promise you that much, Hal.'

⋆   ⋆   ⋆

A couple of weeks later, after the Narcs had wrapped it up, Randall bought me a pizza and told me how they did it.

'It wasn't too tough with what you gave them, Hal. To identify and locate the kid's boss, the Narcs figured their best bet was to put a tail on the kid on Saturday morning, after he'd picked up his weekly load of books at your library. They reasoned that whoever the adult pusher was, he'd certainly want his personal possession of the heroin to be as short a time as possible before handing it over to his holder. So it seemed a good bet that the pusher got his weekly supply of smack from his dealer at about the same time on Saturday morning that the kid would show up with the books to distribute it in. And that's the way it worked. The kid led them right to the pusher.'

'Great!' I said. 'Who was it?'

'A flashy twenty-year-old who lives in the same tenement as Jasper and his mother. On the top floor. Kind of a local idol with the ghetto kids. Turned out later he's Jasper's cousin.'

'That's all there was to it?' I asked incredulously. 'Just follow the kid and pick up his cousin?'

'Not quite. The Narcs couldn't be absolutely sure the cousin was their man. The kid could have stopped to see him for any number of reasons, of course.'

I nodded.

'After about fifteen minutes in his cousin's place, the kid comes out and goes back downstairs to his own pad. And believe it or not, Hal, the kid sits down and starts to read his new library books right through, one after the other. Outside in the alley, the Narc is watching him through the window. By lunchtime, the kid's finished reading maybe five or six books. He puts them in his book-bag, makes himself a Dagwood sandwich — his mother was out working — and goes off to the playground down the street.'

'With the book-bag?'

'With the book-bag. The Narc trailed along. When Jasper got involved in a basketball game, the tail went back to the tenement and — ah — managed to examine the library books the kid hadn't taken with him to the playground.'

I said, 'He had a warrant, I hope.'

Randall shrugged. 'Anyway, he found a glassine envelope of heroin in the pocket of every book — about a ten-dollar packet, he said. So that put the finger on the cousin with no possibility of mistake. You see? No heroin in the books when they left the library. And every book stuffed with it after Jasper's visit to his cousin.'

I nodded again. 'Then what?'

'Then the Narc went back to the playground and kept a cozy eye on Jasper Jones. Three times during the afternoon, the kid was called out of the basketball game by men who passed him a coin — and some code name, probably — and received, in return, one of Jasper's library books. The cousin never showed at all.'

'Directing traffic from a distance.'

'Right.' Randall continued placidly, 'At six o'clock it's getting dark. The kid goes home and eats dinner with his mother, who's now home from work. And that's what the pattern was like all week for Jasper Jones — passing out library books on demand to users at school, at the playground, or at home.'

I shook my head. 'An eleven-year-old kid!'

'Listen,' Randall said softly, 'don't feel too bad about Jasper Jones. Lieutenant Logan told me that while his man was staked out at the Gardenia Street playground, he saw a guy take delivery of two bundles of smack from a little girl who was jumping rope on the sidewalk. She couldn't have been more than six or seven years old. And when this guy called to her, she rolled up the sleeve of her sweater and revealed a lot of packages of heroin taped to her arm. He took what was needed, and the little girl rolled down her sleeve and went back to jumping rope.'

I found myself hoping with an almost feral ferocity that somehow, some way, justice would be visited on the depraved animals who recruited little children to do their dirty work for them. I said harshly, 'Did they nail Jasper's cousin?'

'Yeah. Relax.'

'When did they make the arrest?'

'Last Saturday morning. The Narcs hit him after he'd got his supply from his dealer, and before Jasper arrived with his library books to take it off his hands. The cousin's going down for life, Hal.'

I sighed. 'I hope to God he gets the whole treatment!' I hesitated. 'What about the kid?'

'Jasper?' Randall's sulfur-yellow eyes held a spark of something that could have been sympathy. 'Lieutenant Logan, at my request, released Jasper Jones into the custody of his mother.'

Suddenly I felt fine. 'Let me buy you a beer, Lieutenant.'

He gave me a calm, cool stare. 'Gladly,' he said, 'and you can pay for the pizza, too, if you feel all that grateful.'

I paid for the pizza.

3

The Honeycomb of Silence

I found a public telephone booth on the apron of a gas station two blocks away from Benton's house. I pulled into the service station, parked out of the way of possible pump traffic, and entered the stuffy booth, groping in my pocket for change.

It was a hot, bright morning in August — a Tuesday, I remember — and I was sweating even before I closed myself into the booth.

Instead of dialing the emergency number, I called Headquarters and asked for Lieutenant Randall of Homicide. He was my former boss. I hadn't seen him or heard from him in several months, so I figured this was a pretty good chance to say hello.

Randall picked up his phone and said, 'Yeah?' in a bored voice. 'Lieutenant Randall.'

'Hal Johnson,' I said. 'Remember me?'

'Vaguely,' he answered. 'Aren't you that sissy cop from the public library?'

'You *do* remember me,' I said. 'How nice. Are you keeping busy these days, Lieutenant?'

'So-so.' He paused. Then, with an edge of suspicion, 'Why?'

'I think I may have stumbled across a job for you, Lieutenant.'

'You always were papa's little helper,' Randall said. 'What kind of job?'

'I think a man's been murdered at 4321 Eastwood Street.'

'You *think* a man's been murdered?'

'Yes. I went there just now to collect an overdue library book, and when nobody answered the doorbell, I took a quick look through the living-room curtains — which weren't drawn quite tight — and I saw a man lying on the floor in front of the TV set. The TV was turned on. I could hear the sound and see the picture through the window.'

'Did you go inside?'

I was shocked. 'After all you taught me? Of course not. I didn't even try the door.'

'So the guy didn't hear you ring the doorbell on account of the TV noise,' said Randall hopefully. 'He's tired. He's lying on the floor to relax while he watches his favorite soap opera.'

'Face down? And with all that blood on the back of his shirt?'

Randall sighed. '4321 Eastwood?'

'Right.'

'I'll send somebody to check it out. What name did you have for that address?'

'Robert Fenton. I hope he's not the guy on the floor, though.'

'Why?'

'Because if it's Fenton, he owes the library a fine of two dollars and twenty cents on his overdue library book.'

'You're breaking my heart,' Randall said. 'Where are you calling from?'

'A payphone two blocks away. Do you want me to go back and wait for your boys?'

'No. Thanks all the same.' His voice became bland. 'If it's a murder, we'll try to handle it all by ourselves this time, Hal. Aren't there some kids somewhere with overdue picture books you can track down today?'

*   *   *

Randall telephoned me back at home that evening. His call came just as I was taking my initial sip of my first cold martini before dinner. I hadn't even decided yet whether to go out to eat, or to finish up the meatloaf left over from the pitiful bachelor Sunday dinner I'd cooked for myself two days before.

Randall said, 'The guy wasn't watching a soap opera, Hal. He was dead.'

'He looked dead,' I said. 'Was he murdered?'

'We think so — the lock on the back door had been forced, and he'd been shot in the back and there wasn't any gun around.'

'Oh,' I said. 'And was he Robert Fenton?'

'According to the evidence of his landlord, his neighbors, and the bartender at Calhoun's Bar down the street, he was. The bartender ought to know because she went out with him a few times. It seems he was a bachelor, living alone.'

'A lady bartender?'

'Yeah. Not bad-looking, either,' said Randall, 'if you go for bottle-blondes with false eyelashes.'

I didn't rise to that. At this point, I'm still waiting for Ellen Crosby, the girl at the library's check-out desk, to tell me she'll marry me or else to get lost.

'How about Mr. Fenton's library book, Randall?' I said. 'Can I have it?'

'Which one was it? There were several library books scattered around the living room.'

'I'll have to look up the title. Fenton probably borrowed the others recently, and they're not overdue yet. Anyway, can I have them back to clean up his library record?'

'Why not?' Randall agreed. 'Stop by tomorrow and I'll have them for you.'

'Thanks,' I said. 'I'll be there.'

Lieutenant Randall was as good as his word. When I got to his office next morning about eleven, he had a stack of library books waiting for me.

'You have any suspects yet?' I asked him.

He shook his head. 'Fenton had only lived there for a year, according to his landlord. And nothing in the house showed where he'd been before. As far as we've been able to discover, he has no relatives or friends in town except the blonde bartender in Calhoun's Bar.'

I said, 'Who's looking for friends? It's an enemy who killed him, presumably.'

Randall grunted. 'We haven't turned up any of those, either.'

'Funny. No friends, no relatives, no enemies?'

'And no job either.'

'Fenton was unemployed?'

'A gentleman of leisure. With private means. That's what he told the blonde bartender, anyway.'

'Hell, that's what *I'd* tell a blonde bartender too,' I said. 'That doesn't mean it's true.'

Randall lit a cigar — if you can call those black ropes he smokes cigars. He said, 'Exactly what did you see through the crack in Fenton's draperies yesterday?'

'Just what I told you. Fenton lying on the floor looking very dead, blood all over the place, the TV set going.'

'You didn't notice anything else?'

'No. I went to call you after one look. Should I have noticed anything else?'

'The joint was a shambles, Hal. Somebody had tossed it. Almost a professional job.'

'The killer?'

'We're guessing so. Looking very hard for something.'

'A prowler,' I suggested, 'looking for dough. Interrupted by Fenton.'

Randall shrugged. 'Maybe. Fenton's wallet was missing. But if so, the prowler overlooked five one-hundred-dollar bills in Fenton's money belt.'

'You wouldn't usually hang around long enough after shooting somebody to make a thorough search of his body, would you?'

Randall shrugged again. I stood up. 'Well, anyway, Lieutenant, thanks for salvaging my library books.' I gathered them up.

'Do you need any help?' he asked. 'You

could rupture yourself.'

I ignored that. 'Have you looked through these books?'

'Sure.'

'Whoever killed Fenton was searching for something,' I said. 'Books make dandy hiding places.'

'We looked, Hal. There's nothing in them.'

'They haven't been searched by an expert until *I* search them,' I said, knowing it would infuriate Randall.

He snorted. 'Well, don't do it here. Get lost, will you?'

I grinned at him and took the books and went on about my business, which is tracing down lost, stolen, and overdue books for the public library. It's a quiet life after working for Randall in Homicide for five years. But I like it. Almost as much as Randall resents it.

When I got back to the library that afternoon about four, I turned in the fines and the books I'd collected on my rounds — all except the books Randall had found in Fenton's living room. These, I took with me to my minuscule office behind the director's spacious one, and began to examine them carefully, one by one.

I examined the card pocket of each book, the space between spine and cover, the paper dustjackets. I checked each book painstakingly for anything hidden between the pages, either loose or attached.

There were eight books in the stack. I was holding the seventh book by its covers, shaking its pages down over my desk to dislodge anything that might possibly have been inserted between the pages, when I struck pay dirt.

Under the fingers of my right hand. I felt a slight irregularity beneath the dustjacket.

We protect the dustjacket of every library book with a transparent jacket cover made of heavy cellophane with a white paper liner. We fit this transparent cover over the book jacket, fold it along the edges to fit the book, and attach the end flaps to the book with paste. It was under one of these end flaps that my fingers encountered a slight ridge that shouldn't have been there — a suggestion of extra thickness. The book was called *Mushroom Culture in Pennsylvania.*

Feeling a tingle of excitement, I worked the pasted edge of the fold-over flap loose from its moorings, pulled it clear of the book cover, and found myself staring down at a crisp fresh one-hundred-dollar bill.

I looked at it for a second or two without touching it, surprised and — yes, mildly elated. As an ex-homicide cop, I knew enough not to handle the bill and chance destroying or smearing any recoverable fingerprints. Yet as a curious library cop, I couldn't resist using a pair of stamp tweezers from my desk drawer to tease the bill aside enough to count the others under it. There were ten of them — all hundreds — crisp, fresh, deliciously spendable-looking. A thousand dollars.

I won't say I wasn't tempted. Funny thoughts ran through my head. *Nobody knows about this money but me,* I thought. *This is a library book, so it's kind of like public property,* I told myself, *and I'm certainly one of the public.* And wasn't there a section of the criminal code that said something about *finders keepers?* However, after a couple of minutes, I'm proud to say that I picked up my telephone and asked the switchboard operator to get me Lieutenant Randall.

★　★　★

I was eating lunch in the library cafeteria the next day when Lieutenant Randall appeared in the cafeteria doorway. He spotted me at once, walked to my table, and slid into a chair.

I said, 'Welcome, Lieutenant. You're just in time to pay my lunch check.'

Randall said, 'Why should I? Because you turned that money over to me? You probably figured it was counterfeit, anyway.'

I stopped, a spoonful of chocolate ice cream halfway to my mouth. 'And was it?'

He shook his head. 'Good as gold. So finish up that slop and let's get out of here where we can talk.'

I went on eating very deliberately. 'First things first,' I said. 'I should think out of common gratitude the police department would pay my cafeteria tab for the help I've given you. It's only a dollar and twenty-three cents.'

'Subornation of a witness,' Randall said. He ostentatiously got one of his black cigars from his pocket and felt for matches.

I said, 'No smoking in here, Lieutenant. Don't you see that sign?'

He gave me a cold stare. 'Who's going to stop me? I outrank the only other cop I see anywhere around.'

'O.K.,' I said with a sigh, 'I'll go quietly.'

I paid my check and we went upstairs to my office. The lieutenant sat down in a straight chair facing me across my desk. I said, 'All right, Lieutenant, you need more help, is that it?'

Randall gave what for him was a humble nod. 'This book business has us talking to ourselves, Hal. We did find out something this morning that has a bearing, we think. Fenton was a man who had a lot of hundred-dollar bills, apparently. His landlord says he always paid his rent with hundred-dollar bills. The bartender at Calhoun's Bar says he sometimes paid for his drinks by breaking a hundred-dollar bill. And he had five hundred-dollar bills in his money belt when we found him.'

'So the fact that the money in the library book was in hundreds too makes you think they were intended for Fenton?'

'It seems likely. And possibly they were from the same source as the others he had.'

'And also transferred via library book?'

'Could be.' Randall frowned. 'But I can't figure out how whoever hid the money in the book could be sure Fenton got it. Anybody could borrow the damn book once it came back to the library with the money in it . . . '

'Not if Fenton had put in a reserve for it.' I said. 'Then, when it came back to the library, we'd send him a postcard and hold the book for him for three days.'

'Well,' said Randall, 'that could explain Fenton's end of it. But how about the guy *paying* the money? How'd he know what library book Fenton wanted him to put it in?'

I leaned back and thought about that. At length I said, 'There's only one way I can see. Fenton could call the library and put in a reserve on that book in the other guy's name. Then, when the book was available, we'd automatically notify the other guy that the book he'd reserved was in. And he'd know that was the book Fenton meant for him to put the money in.'

Randall nodded. 'And meanwhile Fenton calls in his own reservation on the same book so he'll be sure to get it when it's returned to the library?'

'Yeah,' I said. 'That could work.'

'It's pretty complicated. Who knows enough about how a library operates to dope out a system like that?'

'I do, for one,' I answered modestly. 'And maybe Fenton did too.'

Randall brooded. 'Say you're right about it. Then how come the money was still in the book? Why didn't Fenton take it out as soon as he got home from the library?'

'What time does the M.E. figure he was killed?'

'Sixteen to eighteen hours before you found him.'

'O.K. That's about the time he might have got home from the library with his books — around cocktail time, let's say. So maybe he mixed himself a drink and turned on the TV before he removed the money from the book? And he was killed before he had a chance to retrieve it.'

Randall made a noncommittal gesture with his hands. He fiddled with his unlit cigar. 'The whole thing smells more and more like blackmail to me,' he said. 'There's only one reason I can think of for Fenton to devise this crazy pay-off method, Hal. To conceal his identity from whoever he was blackmailing. It's a more elaborate scheme than the usual trick of renting a post-office box under a false name and having your blackmail payments mailed to you there.'

'You can stake out a post-office box and see who comes to collect mail from it,' I said. 'But there's no way you can tell who's going to borrow a library book from the public library after you return it. Besides, we circulate more than one copy of most of our books. How are you going to keep track of the particular copy you hid your money in?'

In a deceptively innocent voice, Randall asked, 'How many copies of *Mushroom Culture in Pennsylvania* does the library have in circulation?'

'One,' I admitted, grinning at him. 'There are some books we have only a single copy of. And maybe that's worth noting. *Mushroom Culture in Pennsylvania* was the only one of Fenton's library books that doesn't have two or more copies in stock.'

'So what?'

'So by reserving an unpopular one-copy book for his blackmail victim, Fenton made sure there wouldn't be a long wait before he got his money.'

'The devil with that,' said Randall irritably. 'All a guy would have to do to find out who borrowed a certain book is ask your librarian to look it up for him. Right?'

'Wrong. That's against the rules — as is giving out information about who's on the waiting list for books that have been reserved. Our system works on card numbers, not names.'

'I know that, but when you issue a library card to somebody you take a record of his name and address, don't you?'

'Sure,' I said easily. 'But matching the names to the numbers is the trick. Once a book you've borrowed is returned to the library by its next borrower, you can tell by the date card in its pocket the card renumber of the person who borrowed the book after you did, but not the person's name.'

'There must be plenty of ways to crack *that* crummy system,' Randall commented acidly.

I shrugged. 'Our master file of cardholders' names and numbers is kept out at the main desk.'

'Locked up? In a safe?'

'Just a simple file cabinet,' I said, deadpan. 'I suppose somebody might gain unauthorized access to it.'

Randall said with contempt, 'Child's play.'

'For example?'

'I could hide in the stacks some evening until the library closes and the staff goes home. Then I'd have all night to locate your damn file and milk it.'

'That's very good,' I complimented him. 'Right off the top of your head, too.'

The lieutenant jumped up. 'Let's stop fooling around, Hal. Lead me to this master file of yours. You have authorized access to it, right? So if we can nail down the name and address of the person who borrowed *Mushroom Culture* just before Fenton, we may have our killer.'

'Wait a minute,' I said. 'Say we're right about this being blackmail, and your blackmailee figures out Fenton's identity through his card number. He goes out to Fenton's house Monday afternoon, breaks in through the back door, and is turning the joint upside down looking for whatever blackmail evidence Fenton is holding over him. O.K. Fenton comes home from the library unexpectedly, interrupts him, and gets shot for his pains. His killer is sure to see *Mushroom Culture* among the library books Fenton is bringing home. If he'd hidden a thousand bucks of his money in that book just a day or so before, wouldn't he take his money back? Why did he leave it in the book for me to find afterward?'

Randall said impatiently, 'How should I know? Give me his name and I'll ask him! Come on, Hal. Move!'

I reached into the center drawer of my desk and pulled out a card.

'I just happen to have the information you want right here, Lieutenant. I looked it up this morning.'

'Why didn't you say so?'

'I wanted you to ask me, nice and polite,' I said. 'Because you assured me last Tuesday morning that you wouldn't need any help from me this time. Remember?'

Randall didn't give an inch. 'How was I supposed to know the murdered man would turn out to be another damn library expert?' he said.

He took the card and read the name out loud. 'Samuel J. Klausen.' And the card number: 'L-1310077.'

When he left, he had the grace to throw a 'Thanks, Hal' over his shoulder.

I felt smug.

* * *

My smugness vanished when Randall called me at the library the following noon. 'Is this the resident library expert?' he greeted me.

'It's too late for compliments. Did you arrest Mr. Samuel J. Klausen?'

'No way. He was a washout, Hal. He's no more a murderer than I am.'

I was disappointed but not surprised. 'Not even a blackmailee?'

'Oh, yes, he admits to being blackmailed. He broke wide open when I told him we'd found his fingerprints on the money in the library book.'

'Did you find his prints?'

Randall coughed. 'We found fingerprints, yes. We didn't know they were his until he admitted the blackmail payments.' Randall coughed again. 'Anyway, he readily admitted he was paying off somebody in hundred-dollar bills concealed in library books — but until we told him, he didn't know it was Fenton. He claims he didn't know Fenton from Adam's off ox.'

'Did he tell you how the book thing worked?'

'About the way we worked it out. A year ago, Klausen got a print of a very compromising photograph in the mail, no return address; then a phone call from a man threatening to send the picture to Klausen's wife unless he paid him hush money. When Klausen agreed to do so, the man asked him if he had a library card, and set up the library-book pay-off system.'

'What did Fenton have on Klausen?' I asked curiously.

'None of your business.'

'Excuse me,' I said. 'Is it any of my business why you're so sure Klausen didn't kill Fenton, despite his denials?'

'Klausen has a cast-iron alibi for Monday evening when Fenton was shot.'

I clicked my tongue against my teeth. 'Too bad. Cast-iron, you say?'

'Klausen was making a dinner speech to a gathering of insurance brokers in Baltimore, five hundred miles away, when Fenton caught it. We've checked it out.'

'That's pretty cast-iron, all right,' I said. 'So what's next?'

'Back to the drawing board, I guess.

Unless you've got some more brilliant suggestions.'

'Let me think about it,' I said.

'Nuts to that. *I* do the thinking from here in. You just give me the library jazz when I need it, O.K.? So here's something to start with. Suppose Fenton was blackmailing somebody else besides Klausen, which seems fairly likely, and using the same library-book method of collecting his money? Would he use the same books he did for Klausen, or different ones?'

'Different ones,' I said promptly. 'Even if he didn't screw up his timetables, our people would think it was queer if he reserved the same books for himself more than once.'

'Check. Now, here's another little thought for you. Did you happen to notice, Hal, that none of the eight books we brought in from Fenton's house was overdue?'

He whistled a few bars from 'Tea for Two' under his breath, while he waited for me to realize the full enormity of my oversight. Then, 'You did tell me, didn't you, Hal, that you were calling on Fenton last Tuesday to collect an overdue book?'

I abased myself. 'Yeah, I did. And Lieutenant, I'm sorry. I guess finding the money in *Mushroom Culture* drove everything else from my mind, including that overdue book.'

'Well, well,' Randall said softly.

I said, 'You want me to go out and jump off a bridge or something?'

'Not just yet.' The more apologetic I became, the more cheerful Randall sounded. 'Not till you tell me the title of that overdue book.'

'Hold on,' I said. 'I'll look it up.' I checked my overdue lists. 'It's a book called *The Honeycomb of Silence* by somebody named Desmond.'

'Another one I'm just dying to read,' Randall cracked. 'So I'm on my way right now out to Fenton's house to find it. It might tell us something if we're lucky.'

'You want the name of the person who borrowed it before Fenton?' I offered.

'Not till I find the book.' He hung up with a crash.

I got back to the library after my

afternoon calls about five-thirty. There was a message on my desk to call Randall. I called him and he said, 'I'll take that name now, Hal.'

'You found the book?'

'Between the back of the TV set and the wall. It obviously slipped down there after Fenton took the money out of it, and he forgot to return it to the library. Hence, it was overdue.'

'After he took the money out of it,' I repeated. 'So it was another of Fenton's pay-off books?'

'Shut up and give me the name of the cardholder before Fenton. And let's hope he doesn't have an alibi like Klausen's.'

I read him the name and address from the master file card: W. G. Crowley, 1722 Plumrose Street.

★   ★   ★

I knew everything had worked out all right because on Tuesday of the following week, Lieutenant Randall called and offered to buy me a dinner at Al's Diner, provided the total cost of my repast didn't exceed a dollar and twenty-three cents.

At Al's Diner, he was seated in a back booth waiting for me. He had a look of work-well-done on his face, and a beer on the table before him. 'Sit down,' he invited me expansively, 'and join me in a beer. I hope you don't want a salad with your hamburger, however. Salads are thirty-five cents in this joint.'

'Never touch them,' I said, sliding into the seat across from him. 'But I'll take the beer.' He signaled to the waitress. When she brought my beer, we told her we'd order dinner later.

I took a sip of my beer and said to Randall, 'Did you snaffle W. G. Crowley?'

He nodded.

'And he's your murderer?'

He nodded again. 'Murderer, bank robber, dope pusher. And also, I'm sorry to say, an ex-cop.'

I stared at him. 'Are you serious?'

'He used to be a member of the narcotics squad of the Los Angeles Police Department, under a different name — his real one — James G. Crawford. He's a security guard at the First

National Bank here. And that's where the bank robbery charge comes in. The guy had the nerve to steal the hundred-dollar bills he was paying Fenton from his own bank! How do you like that for resourcefulness?'

'If he's all that resourceful,' I suggested, 'he's probably resourceful enough to walk away from your murder indictment too. You did say he was Fenton's killer, didn't you?'

'No question about it. Open and shut, as the TV cops say. And don't worry, we've got him hogtied. He'll never walk away from anything again.'

'Good,' I said. 'What do you mean, *again*?'

'He was suspended from the LAPD, charged with pushing the dope that his own narc squad appropriated in raids. And before the grand jury could come up with an indictment, he jumped bail and left town permanently. Disappeared. Now he's a bank guard here in town calling himself Crowley.'

'And you're certain he killed Fenton?'

'With his very own police positive,' said

Randall. 'The .38 he carries under his arm every day as a guard at the First National.' Randall held up a hand as I opened my mouth to speak. 'And how, you are about to ask,' he said, 'do we know that? Well, we found three of his fingerprints *under* the flap of the book about honeycombs. And the same three prints on one of the hundred-dollar bills in Fenton's money belt. And the same three prints again among those on the butt of Mr. Crowley's gun. Isn't that enough?'

'Not enough to convict him. And you know it.'

His yellow eyes emitted a gleam of satisfaction. 'Well, then, how about this? Our ballistics boy tells us the bullets taken out of Fenton's body were fired by Crowley's gun. And Crowley has zilch in the way of an alibi for the time of Fenton's murder. And he also, of course, had a good solid motive for killing Fenton.'

'What did Fenton have on him?' I asked.

'Probably just the knowledge that Crowley was really Crawford: the indicted, dope-pushing LA cop who disappeared without leave. Fenton could have landed him in jail for quite a spell by disclosing his whereabouts to the LA police.'

I said, 'I don't get it. If that was the case, what was Crowley looking for when he searched Fenton's house? All he needed to do was kill Fenton to protect himself.'

'I've got two theories on that.' Randall said. 'One: he was trying to make the murder look like what we originally thought it might be — the work of a casual prowler. Or, two — ' Randall's unblinking sulfur-colored stare was amused. ' — maybe Crowley was thinking of taking over Fenton's customers, and *collecting* a little black-mail money for a change instead of paying it out.'

He paused, and I said, 'The first theory might be possible. But what gave rise to the second? Your overactive imagination?'

'We found something interesting in Crowley's apartment,' Randall replied.

Dutifully, I asked, 'What?'

'The negative of the compromising photograph that Fenton used on Klausen,' Randall said, 'all neatly labeled with Klausen's name and address.'

'Well, well,' I said. 'For an ex-cop, Crowley was pretty bright, wasn't he?'

'You can't insult me tonight,' Randall said comfortably. 'Finish your beer and let's order.'

'Not yet. I still don't get it.'

'Get what?'

'How Fenton knew that Crowley was the fugitive Crawford.'

Randall shrugged. 'What difference does that make? Accident, I imagine. Fenton just happened to see Crowley in the bank one day, probably, and recognized him.'

'You mean Fenton knew him in Los Angeles?'

'Maybe. Or at least knew what he looked like.'

'All right. My next question is the real puzzler to me. How did you find out that both Crowley and Fenton came from Los Angeles? You didn't know fact one about Fenton or Crowley, the last I heard.'

He gave a negligent wave of his hand. 'Just good solid routine police work, sonny. After Klausen pointed us toward Los Angeles.'

'Klausen!' I said, confused. 'He pointed

you toward LA?'

'Didn't I mention it?' Randall was complacent. 'The — ah — indiscretion for which Klausen was being blackmailed by Fenton occurred at a convention Klausen attended last year in Los Angeles.'

'Oh,' I said.

'LA gave us a rundown on Fenton, too. They'd had him up out there for extortion once, and for peddling porno films twice, and he walked away each time without a scratch. A very cagey fellow. Incidentally, his Los Angeles record showed that while he was in high school, he worked summers at the public library.'

I finished my beer. 'Very, very neat, Lieutenant. May I offer my congratulations? And we may as well order now.'

As he signaled for the waitress, he seemed so pleased with himself that I couldn't resist saying, 'All the same, you'd never have got to first base on Fenton's murder, may I modestly point out, if I hadn't found that money in *Mushroom Culture*.'

'That's not necessarily so,' said Randall judiciously. 'But it's possible you're right, of course.'

'Wherefore,' I said, 'may I please have a tossed salad with my hamburger?'

Randall grinned. 'Well — O.K. Just this once, I guess I can throw caution to the winds.'

'And speaking of financial matters,' I went on, 'what are you planning to do with that five hundred bucks you found in Fenton's money belt?'

'In default of any known relatives or heirs, I thought I'd turn it over to the Police Benevolent Fund.'

'You can't do that,' I said. 'At least not all of it.'

'No?' He bristled. 'Why not?'

'Because part of that money is mine.'

He looked at me as though I'd lost my mind. 'Yours? What do you mean, yours?'

'Now whose memory is failing?' I said. 'Didn't I tell you last Tuesday that Fenton owes me an overdue fine of two dollars and twenty cents on *The Honeycomb of Silence*?'

4

The Jack O'Neal Affair

You'd think that chasing down missing and overdue books for the public library would be pretty dull and unexciting work, wouldn't you? Most of the time, it is. But occasionally my job gets me into situations that are very far from dull and unexciting, believe me.

Like the Jack O'Neal affair.

It started off like any other call to collect an overdue book. The address was 1218 King Street. King Street's in the East End, a couple of blocks south of the Crossroads intersection, in a still-decent but deteriorating neighborhood of sixty-year-old houses. Number 1218 seemed to be better cared for than the houses that flanked it on either side. Its small lawn was neat and close-cropped and the house had been freshly painted quite recently.

I parked my car at the curb, walked up the short cemented driveway to the house, and rang the bell. A white-haired, pleasant-faced woman answered the door.

I said. 'Is this the O'Neal residence?'

She gave me a big smile and said, 'Yes, it is,' and waited for me to explain myself.

'I'm Hal Johnson from the public library, Mrs. O'Neal.' I showed her my identification card. 'I've come to collect an overdue library book that was borrowed five and a half weeks ago by John C. O'Neal. Is that your husband?'

She shook her head. 'My son,' she said. 'Jack. I'm sorry, but he's not here right now, Mr. Johnson. He's at work.' Then she added with a note of pride, 'He's a city fireman, you know.'

'Oh,' I said, 'that's what I wanted to be when I was a kid. A fireman. I never made it, though. I — '

She interrupted me. 'Yes, Jack's a fireman. And he really loves the job. It's his whole world, really. He never showed the slightest interest in getting married or anything like that, can you believe it? He mopes and sulks around here every

Friday — that's his day off — as though he'd much rather be working down at the firehouse. But you can't work seven days a week, I tell him, you have to have free time.'

'I need all the free time I can get,' I said, trying to head off any further comment about John O'Neal the fireman. 'For instance, if you could just give me your son's overdue library book, Mrs. O'Neal, I wouldn't have to make another trip out here for it. You son has forgotten that he has the book, I suppose, although we did send him a postcard reminding him it's overdue.'

Mrs. O'Neal stepped back and held the door open wider. 'Oh,' she said, flustered and apologetic, 'please come in, Mr. Johnson. I'll see if I can find it for you. Jack would forget his head if it wasn't fastened on.'

I followed her into a living room that was as neat and manicured as the lawn outside. An expensive television set stood in one corner, next to a built-in bookcase. Avocado shag carpeting stretched from wall to wall. The overstuffed sofa and easy chairs wore tasteful slipcovers in harmonizing prints. The lampshades looked almost new.

'What's the name of the book?' Mrs. O'Neal asked.

I consulted my list. '*War and Peace* by Leo Tolstoy.'

'Sit down for a minute,' Mrs. O'Neal said. 'I'll see if it's in Jack's bedroom upstairs. That's where he usually does his reading.' Her voice faded as she ascended the stairs to the second floor.

Instead of sitting down, I wandered over to the bookcase beside the TV set and scanned the titles on the shelves, thinking that Jack O'Neal might have absent-mindedly stowed *War and Peace* there after he finished reading it.

War and Peace wasn't there. As I turned away, an outsize scrapbook lying horizontally on top of the books on the bottom shelf caught my eye. It had the word 'FIRES' lovingly hand-lettered on its cover in old English script. Evidently the work of Jack O'Neal, the fireman who loved his work.

Idly, I picked up the scrapbook and

leafed through it while I waited for Mrs. O'Neal to return with *War and Peace. FIRES* was an apt title. The scrapbook contained nothing but clippings from local newspapers describing a number of newsworthy fires that had occurred over the past few years in the city. The articles were illustrated with photographs of the fires in progress, and of the smoking ruins afterward. Most of the fires in the book — only half a dozen — I remembered reading about. A furniture warehouse. The fancy home of a local lawyer. A dry-goods store. A tenement. An Italian restaurant on the North Side that had once been famous for its gnocchi. A florist's warehouse on City Line.

I heard Mrs. O'Neal's thumping footsteps descending the carpeted stairs and returned the scrapbook to its place in the bookcase, thinking it was only to be expected that a fireman who loved his work as much as Jack O'Neal evidently did would keep a record of his most dramatic encounters with the enemy. Personally, I was very glad that I hadn't realized my boyhood dream of becoming a fireman, although it was bad enough to have become a cop. A sissy library cop at that.

'I found it,' Mrs. O'Neal said, handing me the overdue copy of *War and Peace*. 'My, it's a long book, isn't it? Maybe Jack hasn't finished it yet. He isn't a fast reader.' She shook her head fondly. 'But I expect he really just forgot about it, as you say. It was on the floor by his bed, out of sight under the telephone stand.'

'If he hasn't finished reading it,' I said, 'he can borrow it again the next time he comes to the library. So far, he owes us a small fine on it, Mrs. O'Neal. Do you want to take care of that for him?'

'Of course.' She went into the kitchen and reappeared with her purse. 'How much is it?'

I told her and she counted out the exact change. 'I'm sorry Jack's caused you so much trouble, Mr. Johnson. He's so forgetful.' She laughed indulgently. 'He even writes notes to himself to help him remember things.'

'I do that myself.' I smiled at her, holding up my penciled list of overdues.

'Thanks, Mrs. O'Neal.'

I bid her goodbye, put *War and Peace* under my arm, and went down the driveway to my car.

*   *   *

Three days later, I dropped into police headquarters downtown. Since I'd worked there for five years as a homicide detective before switching to library cop, I knew my way around. I climbed the stairs to the gloomy cramped office of Lieutenant Randall, my former boss, and entered without knocking.

Randall was in the act of lighting one of his vicious black stogies, in blatant disregard of the Surgeon General's warnings. He held the flaring match in midair and gave me a dirty look out of his sulfur-colored eyes. 'Well, look who's here,' he greeted me without enthusiasm. 'The famous book detective himself.'

'Hi, Lieutenant,' I said, and sat down without being asked.

Randall puffed on his stogie till it was well alight, then waved out the match.

'What do you want? And make it quick, Hal. I'm busy.'

'Yeah,' I said. 'I can see that.' There wasn't a paper of any kind on his desk.

'What do you want?'

'I'm a public-spirited citizen,' I answered. 'And, as a public-spirited citizen with the community's good at heart, I have come here this morning to help you clean up some unsolved crimes.' I gave him my public-spirited grin.

He gave me his you've-got-just-one-more-minute grin. '*You* can help *me*?' he asked. 'How?'

'By bringing to your attention a couple of murders you completely missed last year. And by pointing out the murderer to you.'

Randall snorted, peering unblinkingly at me through a cloud of rank tobacco smoke. 'How careless of me to miss a couple of murders,' he said blandly. 'What were they?'

'Two derelicts,' I said, 'who had sneaked in out of the freezing weather last November to sleep in an empty building. At least, that's what the newspapers called them. Derelicts.'

Randall came to attention. 'You mean the bums who were burned to death in that empty Ross Street tenement?'

'Yeah,' I said.

'They weren't murdered. They were trespassing in a building that happened to catch fire and incinerate them.'

I shook my head. 'I don't think the building happened to catch fire. I believe somebody deliberately put a torch to it.'

'Arson?' He was patronizing.

I nodded. 'And murder.' He didn't say anything so I went on. 'Even if the arsonist didn't know the bums were holed up inside when he set fire to the building, he's their murderer all the same, isn't he?'

'If there was an arsonist, yes. Nobody has ever suggested that there was one, though — ' Randall sighed. ' — except you.'

'I'm ninety-nine percent sure that there was, Lieutenant. Do you want to get Sandy Castle up here to hear the rest of this?' Sandy Castle heads up the Department's arson squad.

In the old days, when I worked for him,

if I was ninety-nine-percent sure about anything, that was usually enough to convince Randall; and it still was, I guess. He picked up the phone and called Sandy.

While we were waiting, the lieutenant smoked in noncommittal silence for about three minutes. Then he asked casually, 'And who was this murderer, Hal? You said you knew.'

I replied with equal casualness, 'A city fireman named Jack O'Neal.'

That shook him a little. 'A fireman? For God's sake!'

'Ironic, isn't it?'

The door opened and Sandy Castle came in and took the other chair. 'How are you doing, Hal?' he greeted me. 'Back at the old stand?'

'Only temporarily. I've got something I think will interest you, Sandy.'

'So I hear. I'm listening.'

I quickly filled him in on what I'd told Randall. 'I think that tenement fire was set,' I finished.

'He even claims to know who set it,' Randall murmured. 'Don't ask me how.'

'You want it from the beginning?' I said. 'O.K. Last Wednesday I went to collect an overdue library book from a city fireman named Jack O'Neal, who lives with his mother at 1218 King Street. Jack wasn't home, but his mother found the library book for me — on the floor under the telephone extension beside the bed in Jack's upstairs bedroom. While she was upstairs looking for the book, I came across a scrapbook in the living room and glanced through it while I waited. The scrapbook had the word 'FIRES' on the cover, and contained six illustrated newspaper clippings about local fires. The Ross Street tenement fire was one of them.'

Castle looked puzzled. 'Nothing funny about that, Hal. A fireman could keep a scrapbook of fires like a writer keeps a scrapbook of reviews. I've personally known a dozen — '

I held up a hand. 'Wait a minute, Sandy. I'm not finished.'

'Let him talk,' Randall interjected. 'He loves to talk.'

'There were only six clippings in the scrapbook, Sandy. The fires were spread over a period of about three years. And we've had a lot more than six newsworthy fires in this town in the last three years, haven't we?'

'So what?' Castle still looked puzzled. 'Your fireman Jack O'Neal just keeps clippings on the fires that *he* helped to fight. It's natural.'

I shook my head. 'That's what I thought at first, too. Until I found out that Jack O'Neal works at Station 12 and Station 12 wasn't called for any of the fires in his scrapbook.'

Castle said, 'How the hell did you find *that* out?'

'A telephone call to O'Neal's mother. Reading O'Neal's fire clippings in the back issues of the papers. The fire companies involved in fighting each fire were mentioned. No Station 12. Don't you find that odd?'

'Maybe,' Castle admitted. 'You got anything else?'

'Yes. All the fires in O'Neal's scrapbook happened on a Friday.'

'What's that got to do with anything?'

'Friday is O'Neal's day off.'

They both looked at me as though I'd lost my mind. 'You think that's significant, I take it,' Castle said.

I shrugged. 'When taken in connection with some other suggestive items.'

'Like what?' Randall said.

I said with false humility, 'I know how you feel about library cops and library books, Lieutenant, so I hate to bring up the subject. However, I will this time because I think there's an interesting inference to be drawn from the books Jack O'Neal has been reading.'

'Stop with the fancy talk,' Randall grunted. 'Just tell us.'

'I'm trying to. The book I collected from O'Neal was *War and Peace*. Combined with what I saw in O'Neal's scrapbook, it gave me an idea. I looked up the titles of the books O'Neal has borrowed from the library since he got his card several years ago. There were only five of them, so I guess I have to believe his mother that he's a slow reader. Can you guess what the five books were?'

Randall said sardonically, 'I can't wait to hear.'

I ticked them off on my fingers. '*War and Peace. Gone With the Wind. The Life and Death of Joan of Arc. Slaughterhouse-Five. The Tower.* You see what I'm getting at?'

Randall looked blank.

Sandy Castle said, 'Let me guess. I saw *War and Peace* on television. And *Gone With the Wind.* The books all have one thing in common, right? A big fire scene?'

'You amaze me, Sandy,' I said. 'But you're dead right. For his light reading at home, Jack O'Neal chooses books with graphic fire scenes in them. And his mother told me he's so nuts about his job that he wishes he could work seven days a week.' I looked at them quizzically. 'Wouldn't you say the man is definitely keen on fires?'

'Maybe,' Castle conceded, 'but that doesn't make him a torch, Hal.'

'Granted.'

'Nor a murderer,' Lieutenant Randall put in. He fixed his yellow eyes on me and said, 'Come on, Hal, what hard evidence do you have? You must have something better than this jazz you've been feeding us. You wouldn't have worked your dainty

121

fingers to the bone reading all those newspaper clippings because of a mere passing suspicion. So what is it?'

'Let me ask you a question first. Didn't a big hardware store burn to the ground last Friday on the South Side?'

'Sure. Bartlett's Hardware,' Castle said promptly.

'And what was last Friday's date?'

'That's two questions,' Castle said. 'Last Friday was the eighteenth. Why?'

'Because I found a penciled note in O'Neal's overdue library book,' I replied.

Randall pounced. 'Saying what?'

'Saying, and I quote, 'O.K. Bart's 18th.' Which meant absolutely nothing to me until I read about the Bartlett fire in Saturday's paper.'

Randall said brusquely, 'Let's see it.'

'The note? I can't. I threw it away. But that's what it said: 'O.K. Bart's 18th.''

'Why didn't you tell us about this note right off, instead of going through all this other drivel?' Randall demanded testily.

My real reason was just to needle Randall. So I lied a little. 'I wanted to give you the sequence and the coincidences

122

just as I got them,' I said sweetly. 'So you'd be able to put together just as I finally did, all the little facts that seem to add up to one big fact: namely, that Jack O'Neal is an arsonist and a murderer.' I turned to Sandy Castle. 'Is there any suspicion of arson in the Bartlett fire?'

'Not so far. The investigation is still going on, Hal. The fire marshal is certain that the fire originated in a paint storage closet in the store's basement. Spontaneous combustion. And I'm inclined to think he's right.'

'Was the owner of the hardware store in town last Friday?' I asked Castle.

'Bartlett?' He gave me a slanting look. 'No. He was with his family at the seashore for the weekend. You're thinking alibi, aren't you, Hal?'

I shrugged. 'Here's the list of the other fires in O'Neal's scrapbook.' I handed it to him. 'I wonder where the owners of those buildings were when their property burned.'

'I'll check,' said Castle.

Lieutenant Randall's mind began to click, smooth and easy and well-oiled as usual. I could almost hear it. He said, 'This note was in O'Neal's library book, you say, which his mother found beside his bed. Did you say there was a telephone extension beside his bed?'

'That's what his mother told me.'

He nodded. 'So you figured somebody phoned O'Neal to torch Bartlett's store last Friday, and O'Neal wrote down the instructions and put them in his library book.'

'I think that's what happened. O'Neal's mother said Jack had such a rotten memory he often wrote notes to himself as reminders.'

Castle said slowly and heavily, 'My department runs into a dozen wild-eyed nuts a year who get their jollies out of fires instead of sex or drugs. They usually act on their own, though, and on impulse, setting fires indiscriminately. This O'Neal of yours, if you're right about him, isn't like that. He's torching buildings to *order* on certain specified dates.'

'Ah,' I said. 'Now you've got it. But to whose order? That's the question.'

Randall broke in. 'Thanks for the tip,

Hal,' he said, rising from his battered swivel chair and crushing out his stogie in his ashtray. 'We'll take it from here.'

'Good,' I said, standing up too. 'Don't be too rough on O'Neal's mother if you can help it, O.K.? And let me know how you come out, will you? I'm keeping a scrapbook of my own.'

'On what?' asked Castle.

'On the crimes I solve for Lieutenant Randall,' I said.

★   ★   ★

The newspapers called it the biggest arson racket in the history of the state. Thirteen of our local citizens — including merchants, property owners, a lawyer, a real-estate agent, a fire marshal, and, of course, Mrs. O'Neal's son Jack — were ultimately tried and convicted on charges of conspiring to burn property with the intent of defrauding insurance companies. When all the figures were in, they indicated that the arson ring cheated insurance companies of some half million dollars over a period of three years by having properties appraised at inflated values, overinsuring them, then burning the buildings down and filing fraudulent insurance claims.

'I'm sorry we have to go light on your boy O'Neal,' Lieutenant Randall told me. 'He's crazy as a bedbug when it comes to fires, Hal, just as you figured. But he's plenty smart in other ways. Smart enough to plea-bargain himself into a maximum ten-year term for his part in the arsons by agreeing to rat on everybody else in the ring.'

'How did you nail him in the first place?' I asked. 'Nothing I gave you was strong enough to prove he's a torch.'

'Well,' said Randall complacently, 'we didn't have too much trouble. On the presumption that his note in your library book meant what you thought it did, we persuaded Judge Filmer to issue us a search warrant, and we went through O'Neal's home with a fine-tooth comb while he was at work. We turned up a couple of interesting items there.'

'Besides his scrapbook?'

Randall nodded. 'Yep. Item one: a diary

that he kept locked in the drawer of his bedside telephone stand.'

'How lucky can you get?' I said. 'Don't tell me it mentioned the arson jobs?'

'It did. Twice. Sandrini's Florist warehouse. And Bartlett's Hardware. On the exact dates the fires occurred.'

'What did the diary say about them?'

'*Handled S job today for TX.* And *Handled B job today for TX.*'

'That's pretty convincing. But not legal proof. Who's TX?'

'The lawyer whose fancy house burned down.'

I remembered it now, the name I'd read in the newspaper clipping. 'Thomas Xavier! Of course. How many people would have the initials TX?'

'Nobody else connected with *this* case anyway. Knowing that name gave us a little leverage when we braced O'Neal.'

'Xavier is pretty important people,' I ventured.

'Important enough to be the respectable front for the arson ring. The ringleader, in fact. He arranged the torching dates with the property owners, saw that they all had unshakable alibis, gave O'Neal his orders, and set up the insurance claims.'

'Paymaster too?' I asked.

'Yeah. O'Neal says he got five thousand dollars from Xavier for every fire he set. We found his pay for the Bartlett job in O'Neal's locker at the firehouse.'

'Five thousand a job. Not bad. What else did you find besides the diary?'

'A key.' Randall paused ostentatiously to light a cigar. I sighed and asked the question he wanted.

'A key?'

'Yeah. A key to the rear delivery door of Bartlett's Hardware Store.'

'Bartlett's burned to the ground, including that door. How could you tell it was *that* key?'

'There was a little tag tied to it saying 'Rear door, Bartlett's.'' Randall's smile was smug.

I said, 'My God, the guy must have *wanted* to be caught! Where'd you find the key?'

'In a pocket of the slacks his mother told us he wore on the eighteenth, his day off. The eighteenth, get it?'

'I get it. But it's still not enough to have made him sing. Everything against him is purely circumstantial.'

'Not quite,' said Randall. 'As a matter of fact, we kind of implied that an off-duty fireman who knows O'Neal was smooching with his girlfriend in a parked car behind Bartlett's store the night it caught fire. And that this fireman saw Jack O'Neal enter the store by the back door, disappear for a few minutes, then emerge and make tracks away from there just a little time before the fire broke out.'

I clicked my tongue and gave the Lieutenant a shocked stare. 'You mean you told him you had an eyewitness?'

'We didn't *tell* him exactly.' Randall's tone was as bland as cream. 'We merely suggested the possibility in a way that made Jack think it was true. *That's* when he broke wide open.'

'Well,' I said, 'congratulations, Lieutenant. I suppose you've got a solid case against each member of the ring?'

'Airtight.' Randall's cat's eyes regarded me without blinking for a moment. Then he said, 'I told O'Neal about your part in this mess, Hal. About the note you found in his library book that made you suspicious, and so on. And you know what he said?'

'No idea.'

'He said he was sorry we'd caught up to him before he torched just one more building.'

I played straight man again. 'What building?'

'The public library,' said Lieutenant Randall, 'with you in it.'

5

The Reward

I didn't want to waste my time on another fruitless call at Annabel Corelli's home, so I telephoned her at eight-thirty Friday morning.

After two rings, I heard the receiver lifted and a voice said, 'Hello.' The voice was unmistakably female, and it sounded like contralto coffee cream — rich and very, very smooth. It gave me such a jolt of pleasure that for an uneasy moment I felt somehow disloyal to Ellen Corby, one of our librarians, whom I'd been assiduously courting for over a year.

I said, 'Is this Miss Annabel Corelli?'

'Yes.' The way she said it painted an instant image of a tall, Junoesque creature in a string bikini walking along a tropical beach.

'My name is Hal Johnson,' I said, 'and I'm calling about your overdue library book, Miss Corelli. I stopped at your house yesterday to collect it, but you weren't home.'

'I'm almost never home in the daytime, Mr. Johnson. I'm an Argyll Lady. I'm just on my way out to work now.' That figured, I thought, a door-to-door cosmetics lady. With that voice, she ought to be able to sell skin lotion to a porcupine. 'I'm sorry about the book,' she said. 'I'm afraid I let a friend borrow it and then forgot all about it.'

'It's six weeks overdue,' I said, 'and it's a one-week book, so it's costing you a bundle in fines.'

'I'm really sorry, Mr. Johnson.' Her voice caressed me. 'How much do I owe on it?'

I told her.

'Well, how about if I leave the book and the fine in my carport for you so you can pick it up today while I'm out?'

I said, 'Today? But if you've lent the book to a friend — '

'No, today'll be fine,' she said with a laugh. 'The friend I lent it to lives here with me.'

Lucky friend, I thought as I hung up.

I stopped at Miss Corelli's house in the East End in mid-morning. Sure enough, there was the library book — *The Hong Kong Diagram* — on a shelf in the carport, with the exact amount of the fine neatly stacked on top of it. A cornerpost concealed the book and money from anyone not specifically looking for it.

As I put the book on the back seat of my old Ford, it occurred to me that Annabel Corelli must do pretty well as an Argyll Lady. Her house was nothing elaborate, but it was no hovel either — two-story white clapboard with green shutters, and a neat yard attractively planted. And the carport was a two-car job. Maybe Miss Corelli's friend contributed to the budget. I felt a vague sense of regret that I hadn't been able to meet the lady and her exciting voice in person.

That Friday was a busy day for me. By the time I'd made the last call on my overdue list, the hot August afternoon had already gobbled up my usual cocktail hour and was shading rapidly towards dinnertime. I was tired and out of sorts, and I felt sticky. I wanted a long shower and an ice-cold martini, straight up. So, instead of returning to the library to check in my books and fines before I knocked off for the day, I went straight home, luxuriated for twenty minutes in the shower, and had not one but two ice-cold martinis before dining in bachelor loneliness on a double package of frozen chicken chow-mein.

I cleaned up the dishes, listened to the news on television, then turned it off, feeling fidgety and restless and wondering how long it was going to be before Ellen agreed to marry me — or at least let me see her more than two evenings a week, which was my present ration.

Thinking about Ellen reminded me of Annabel Corelli's sexy voice, and that in turn reminded me of her overdue library book, *The Hong Kong Diagram*. It was a relatively new novel of the stolen-nuclear-device-endangers-the-world school, and a suspense blockbuster.

It was full dark now. I went out the back door of my garden apartment into the garage, unlocked the car, and, by the light in the dome, rummaged through the stacks of books in the back seat until I found *The Hong Kong Diagram*.

Have I mentioned that I'm an avid reader? Well, I am. I'll read anything — from coffee-table art books to paperback gothics. I've found that reading's the best way to educate yourself beyond the few basic disciplines you get in college. When I was working as a homicide detective under Lieutenant Randall, before I decided to become a library cop, I'd taken courses in speed reading and memory development. You know how an ambitious rookie in any new job can be an eager beaver? That was me. But, as a matter of fact, the speed reading and memory training come in very handy in my present work, which, as you've probably gathered by now, is to run down overdue and stolen books for the public library.

I figured I could probably zip through *The Hong Kong Diagram* in a few hours. At the very least, it would amuse me until bedtime. I relocked the Ford and went back inside, riffling through the book, looking for anything that might inadvertently have been left between the pages. The shake-out is standard procedure with me when I collect overdue books, and you'd be surprised at some of the items I've discovered. I once found a brand-new hundred-dollar bill in a library book borrowed by an offset printer on the South Side. From the alacrity with which he grabbed the bill and thrust it out of sight, I've always suspected it might have been one he'd printed himself.

There wasn't any hundred-dollar bill in *The Hong Kong Diagram*. There was, however, a list of addresses written in a careless scrawling hand on the back of a sales slip that carried the heading *Argyll Cosmetics*. A memo to herself, I concluded, from Miss Annabel Corelli.

I ran my eye down the half-dozen addresses. They didn't mean anything to me. But they might be important to a door-to-door Argyll Lady. At the very least, I thought, they gave me an excuse for further exposure to Annabel Corelli's golden voice. I dialed her number and waited eagerly for the sound of rich contralto. What I got, after two rings, was a harsh, impatient baritone. 'Yes?'

I said, 'Is Miss Corelli there?'

'Who's calling?'

'Hal Johnson from the public library. I spoke with Miss Corelli this morning.'

'Hang on.'

I hung on, reflecting on the sad fact that Miss Corelli's live-in friend, judging from the depth and proprietary sound of his voice, seemed to be a man — and not another woman, as I'd imagined. Probably a Fuller Brush Man, I thought sourly.

'Hello, Mr. Johnson. Didn't you get your book O.K.? It was gone from the carport when I got home.'

'I got it, Miss Corelli. And thanks. But I found a memo in it, and I thought maybe you'd need it.'

'A memo?' she said with a puzzled lift to that gorgeous voice.

'Yes. A list of addresses written on the back of an Argyll Cosmetics sales slip. Maybe a list of calls you plan to make or something.'

She hesitated a moment. Then, 'Oh,

yes, Mr. Johnson. I recognize it. It *is* a call list, but I don't need it any more. You can throw it away.'

'O.K. I just wanted to be sure it wasn't important.'

'It was terribly nice of you to call about it.'

'Not at all, Miss Corelli,' I said. 'Good night.'

I hung up, tossed the list in the wastepaper basket, and started to read *The Hong Kong Diagram*.

The ads were right; it was a suspense blockbuster. It made me so nervous I couldn't get to sleep until after midnight.

*   *   *

Wild coincidences do happen occasionally in library work like mine, just as I suppose they do in other businesses. I was at my desk in the library the next morning, working on my weekly records, when I got a telephone call from my old boss, Lieutenant Randall of Homicide.

'Hal,' he said, 'do me a favor.' It sounded more like an order than a request, but that was in character for Randall when he was in a hurry.

'Like what?' I asked noncommittally.

'Like saving me a trip to the library. You can get me the information I need quicker than I can — if there is any.'

'What do you need?'

'Any information you can dig up about one of your cardholders named Josephine Sloan. A twenty-seven-year-old woman. Single. A live-in maid. One of your best customers, judging by the stack of borrowed library books in her room.'

'Who has she killed, if I may ask?'

'Nobody that I know of. She was reported missing on the eleventh of this month by her employers, a Mr. and Mrs. Gaither. When the Gaithers got home from a weekend at the shore on that date, she was missing.'

'Along with the family's jewels and silver?'

'No. Nothing was missing except the maid.'

I said, 'Since when have you been switched from Homicide to Missing Persons?'

'I haven't. Josephine Sloan's body was found yesterday afternoon by some kids playing in Gaylord Park. The body, with a badly cracked skull, was stashed under an overhang along the creek bank. It could be a hit-and-run, murder, or any other damn thing except a natural death.'

'Well, in that case,' I said, 'sure. I'll nose around for you. But her employers ought to be able to tell you a hell of a lot more about her than any of our people here.'

'Her employers can't give us anything that helps. We've tried. Since they were away, they don't know anything about her activities that weekend. To hear them tell it, she was a model maid — industrious, efficient, quiet, honest, no known boy-friends.' Randall cleared his throat. 'Which figures, I suppose. She was quite unattractive.'

'I still don't get why you think we can help you, no matter how many library books she read.'

'The post-mortem shows her death had to have occurred that weekend. And we've only got one lousy lead on her movements on Saturday and Sunday.'

A pause.

'Something to do with the library,' I concluded.

'Right. Apparently one of the last things she did before she went missing was to borrow eight books from your library on Saturday the eighth — two weeks ago today. You and your people are probably the last ones to have seen her alive.'

'O.K.,' I said with a deep sigh. 'What do you want me to do?'

'Ask around about her among your Saturday staff and volunteers, find out if anybody knows her. Does anybody remember her coming in on the eighth? Has anybody ever noticed her with a boyfriend at the library? Did she, by some freak of chance, say anything to anybody about her plans for that weekend? Or about her employers being away? You know what I want, Hal. A starting place, that's all.'

'I'll try, Lieutenant,' I said, 'but don't hold your breath.' I took out a pencil. 'Josephine Sloan. Twenty-seven years old.

A spinster. Unattractive. Address?'

'Same as her employers',' said Randall. 'The R. C. Gaithers. Thirty-four, North Linden Drive.'

I took it down. 'I'll be in touch.'

'Thanks, Hal.' We hung up.

That's when the coincidence showed up. As I looked at the address I'd just jotted down on my pad, I realized I'd seen it before very recently. In fact, only last night. On the call-list bookmark left in her overdue library book by Annabel Corelli, the Argyll Lady.

⋆　⋆　⋆

After plenty of questioning, what I got for Randall out of our Saturday staff and volunteers was exactly zero. We have four girls on the checkout desk of the main library, including Ellen, and only one of them had anything of even remote interest to reveal about Josephine Sloan. That was Ellen herself, who, after much thought, said she vaguely remembered checking out some books for the name Sloan on the Saturday morning in question. Beyond that, nobody could remember anything at all. In fact, though two of the other girls and one of our men volunteers were familiar with Josephine Sloan through her frequent visits to the library, not one of them had ever exchanged any more words with her than were necessary to check her books in and out.

Before calling Lieutenant Randall with the bad news, however, I decided, on the basis of that odd coincidence of addresses, to take another look at Annabel Corelli's call list, which should still be reposing in the wastebasket at my apartment. The library closes early on Saturdays. I went straight home, dug the list out, and was pleased to see my memory hadn't let me down on the Sloan address. It was there all right, along with five others — 34 North Linden Drive.

There was something else there too, something that hadn't registered with me the night before when I'd found the list and telephoned Annabel Corelli. I stared at the tiny figures for a moment, then reached for my car keys.

*　*　*

Twenty minutes later, I was sitting across the desk from Lieutenant Randall at the downtown police headquarters. 'You got something for me,' he asked hopefully.

I shook my head. 'I'm sorry. One of the girls remembers Sloan checking out her books on that Saturday, but that's all. And you already knew that.'

Randall sighed. Then he shot me a sleepy look from his cat-yellow eyes. 'So why are you here?'

I told him about the Argyll Lady — about her overdue library book, her live-in boyfriend, her bookmark memo with Josephine Sloan's address on it. He snorted. 'Your Argyll Lady probably called on the Gaither woman to sell her some cosmetics.'

'Right, Lieutenant. But look at the tiny figures under the Gaithers' address there.' I handed him the list and pointed.

Randall peered at them. 'Eight dash eleven,' he read aloud. 'The other addresses all have numbers too. Probably order numbers. Or appointment dates.'

He paused and his eyes narrowed. 'Dates,' he repeated softly. He lit one of his vicious stogies and puffed acrid smoke across his desk in my direction. I coughed. 'Dates,' he murmured again. 'The eighth of the month is approximately when the Sloan girl was killed. And the eleventh is when the Gaithers came home from their weekend and reported her missing. Is that what you're getting at, Hal?'

'Could be,' I said.

'Let's find out.'

Randall was never one to waste time. He called a police clerk into his office, gave him the list of addresses, and told him to get the names and telephone numbers that went with them. While we waited, Randall smoked in silence as I sat on the hard chair and remembered to be grateful I was no longer a homicide cop. Sissy library fuzz or not, it was a lot more restful collecting library books than murderers.

The clerk was back in eight minutes. Randall grunted his thanks, picked up his phone, asked the switchboard for an outside line, and dialed one of the numbers the clerk had just handed him.

After a short wait, a woman answered. 'Mrs. Symons?' Randall said. 'This is the police.' His tone was as bland as vanilla pudding. 'Maybe you can help us. We're investigating a mugging that occurred on your street on the night of — ' He read the tiny numbers under the Symons' address from the call list, ' — either the twenty-seventh or the twenty-eighth of last month. Were you at home those evenings, can you remember?'

Mrs. Symons' voice squawked in the receiver. Randall held the phone far enough from his ear so I could catch her words. They were heavily freighted with indignation. 'A *mugging*!' she said. 'What's the *matter* with the police in this city? It wasn't a mugging at all, as you ought to know very well since you spent a whole morning here at my house investigating it!'

'Oh-oh.' Randall was abject. 'We must have our wires crossed here, Mrs. Symons. If it wasn't a mugging, what was it?'

'Our burglary here! They stole every bit

of sterling silver we had in the house!'

While she paused for breath, Randall repeated his question. 'Were you at home that weekend, Mrs. Symons?'

'At home? Of course not! If it hadn't been Parents' Weekend at our daughter's college, we wouldn't have lost our silver. The house was empty.' Her voice went shrill. 'But I've already *told* all this to one of your men named Leroy! And we haven't heard a *word* from him in almost a month now! *Some* police department! Lucky for us we were insured!'

Randall soothed her. 'I'll ask Detective Leroy to get in touch with you at once. I can't understand this mix-up, Mrs. Symons. I'm very sorry — please believe me.' Mrs. Symons gave the Lieutenant an unlady-like raspberry and hung up abruptly.

Randall grinned. 'Remind you of old times, Hal?' he asked. He picked up the phone again and asked for Detective Leroy in Burglary. While he waited, he talked to me around his stogie. 'We'll take it from here, Hal. Thanks for the lead — '

It was a dismissal. I stood up. 'Thanks aren't enough,' I said. 'I want a reward.'

'Reward?' He glared at me.

'Reward,' I repeated. 'If you decide to interview the Argyll Lady any point during your investigation, I want to be there.'

'What for?'

'So I can see what goes along with that sexy voice,' I said.

*   *   *

The following Friday night, Randall called me after midnight. I'd just come in from a dinner and movie date with Ellen. Randall said, 'You in bed yet?'

'Almost,' I said. 'Why?'

'We've got your Argyll Lady here. If you want to collect that reward come over to headquarters.'

'Now? It's after midnight!'

'So, your police department never sleeps. You coming?'

'What happened?'

'I'll tell you when you get here.' He hung up with a crash.

I sighed. I was tired and sleepy. I wanted to go to bed, not downtown — not even to meet the girl with the sexy voice. After Ellen, Farrah herself would be an anticlimax. But I'd asked for it. I put my jacket and tie back on, and went out to the car.

The lieutenant was alone in his office when I got to headquarters. He smirked at me, and waved me to a chair.

'Couldn't this wait till tomorrow?' I asked.

'You said you wanted to meet her. She may be out on bail tomorrow.'

'Don't tell me *she* killed Josephine Sloan.'

'I won't tell you anything unless you shut up.' He was enjoying himself.

'O.K.,' I said meekly.

'The minute Detective Leroy in Burglary saw that list of your Argyll Lady's,' Randall said, 'we were practically home free. It was just routine from there on.'

'Let me guess. All those addresses had reported burglaries too?'

He nodded. 'Four out of six. All committed when the owners were out of town and the houses were empty. On the dates indicated by the little figures under each address.'

'And silver was stolen from all of them?'

He nodded again. 'With the price of silver today, did you know you can get several grand at the smelter for a set of sterling flatware that retailed for only a few hundred bucks ten years ago? Silver's very big in the B&E business these days.'

'Even a library cop is aware of that,' I said sarcastically. 'So what about Annabel Corelli?'

'In each case, she'd made a sales call at the burglarized house shortly before the burglary took place.'

I grimaced. 'So she *did* set them up. A crooked Argyll Lady. She makes a call, and during a friendly conversation, learns when the lady of the house and her family will be away. She notes the best prospects for a large silver haul, and the dates when no one should be at home.'

Randall blew smoke. 'A neat operation. You got to admire it.'

'I do. But I still don't see how it gets you anywhere with the Sloan murder.'

Randall treated me to one of his unblinking yellow stares. Then he said 'In each of the four burglaries, entry into the house was effected the same way. By means of a hydraulic jack.' I must have looked puzzled, because he went on to explain in a patronizing tone.

'You cushion the pushing head and the footplate of a jack with foam-rubber, and position it horizontally against the edges of a door frame about the level of the lock. When pressure is applied, the jack spreads the doorposts apart enough so the lock and deadbolt tongues are drawn out of their sockets and the door can swing open. When you leave the house with your loot, you release pressure on the jack and the door frames spring back to vertical again, reseating the bolts in their sockets as though they'd never been touched. And the only sign of a break-in having occurred is a couple of shallow pressure marks on the doorposts made by the jack.'

'Well, well,' I said, 'what'll they think of next? I still don't see — ' But as I uttered the words I did see. 'You found the same jack marks on the doorposts of the Gaithers' house.'

'The very same,' said Randall. 'Exact match of the marks on the other four break-ins. Although nothing was reported stolen at that address, remember. Only the disappearance of the maid. Yet a break-in had obviously taken place. Are you beginning to get it now?'

'Yeah. Corelli set up the jobs, and she and her boyfriend probably worked them together. But when they broke into the Gaithers' house, it wasn't empty, as they expected it would be. The maid was there. She probably caught Corelli and friend at the silver chest, and recognized Corelli as the Argyll Lady who called on Mrs. Gaither. So the fat was in the fire, unless — '

Lieutenant Randall nodded. 'Unless something was done to keep the maid from talking. So they did something. They killed her and, leaving the silver behind, they relocked the door, packed the maid into their ear, and hid her body in Gaylord Park, six miles away.'

'Do you have any proof of all this?' I asked.

'Some circumstantial stuff. And when

their lawyer gets here and we can interrogate them, I'm hoping for more. Anyway, we sure as hell have proof they're silver thieves if nothing else. We caught them red-handed, about two hours ago, burgling the last house on your list.' Randall yawned cavernously. 'A blackjack in the boyfriend's pocket could be the Sloan murder weapon. It's at the lab now. And the boys have found a few faint bloodstains on the upholstery of the back seat of Corelli's car that may give us something.'

Randall noted my sour expression and said cheerfully, 'Hal, my boy, you were dead right about your Argyll Lady. She's a real dish. Wait'll you see her.'

He picked up the phone and spoke into it.

* * *

Two minutes later, Annabel Corelli appeared in the doorway escorted by two uniformed cops, one holding each arm. Even without makeup, her auburn hair in a tumbled mess and her clothing in disarray, she was something to see. She was really impressively beautiful — and big. She must have stood almost six feet tall and tipped the scales at a good hundred and sixty-five pounds — every one of them distributed in the proper place.

Randall stood up politely. I also got to my feet. The lieutenant said, 'Miss Corelli, let me present Hal Johnson from the public library. I promised him he could meet you in person if that list of addresses he found in your library book should help us with this case.'

She seemed momentarily taken aback when she heard my name. Then she smiled at me very sweetly. In that unforgettable voice, she said, 'I *am* glad to meet you, Mr. Johnson.'

Trying to hide my embarrassment, I started to mumble something fatuous, I don't remember what. But I didn't get a chance to finish it. Annabel Corelli pulled sharply away from her guards, took two steps toward me, drew back her right arm, and slapped me so hard I fell back against Randall's desk, my head ringing like a church bell.

They hustled her out but I could tell by the frown on Lieutenant Randall's face it was all he could do not to laugh himself sick.

6

The Search for Tamerlane

I was engaged in my bi-weekly proposal of marriage to Ellen Thomas when I got the call.

'I simply can't understand,' I was saying flippantly to Ellen, 'why I am so attractive to other women but not to you. Here I am, a man not too old, not too bad-looking, not too immoral, and probably the best library detective in the business; and my chosen bride, Miss Ellen Thomas of the Public Library, treats me as if I were Joe Unknown from Patagonia. Why is this?'

'I like you, Hal,' Ellen said, not at all flippantly. 'I like you very much indeed. More than I've ever liked another man. But I'm not sure I like you enough to marry you. And spend the rest of my life with you. Even though you *are* a good library detective.'

'And a fine homicide detective before that,' I said.

She began to eat her pineapple upside-down cake. 'Please run that by me again,' she said, her tone changing; 'that bit about your being so attractive to other women.'

We were eating lunch in the cafeteria of the Public Library where we both worked. I took a spoonful of my vanilla ice cream and said with some dignity, 'It's quite true.'

'Name one other woman who finds you all that attractive.'

'Tessie Troutman,' I said. 'A very perspicacious waitress at Carmody's Bar and Grill.'

'Oh, the blonde with the — ' Ellen hesitated. 'The one built out to here?'

'The very same. She's willing to marry me at the drop of a hat.'

'How do you know? Have you asked her?'

'No. And I won't — not until *you* give me a definite answer. But by her ingratiating manner when she brings me my martinis, I can tell that if I *were* to ask

157

her, she'd swoon with pleasure while saying 'Yes' at the top of her lungs.'

'Why?' asked Ellen, scraping industriously at the glutinous remains of her cake. 'Because of your overpowering charm?'

'Not at all,' I said. 'Admittedly, I have no overpowering charm. It's my good looks she fancies. She likes what she sees, you might say.'

'What I might say,' said Ellen, 'is that Tessie — and it's true — has a cast in one eye and sees things slightly out of perspective. Instead, I shall merely be ladylike and tell you that I am honored by your — what is it now? — eighteenth proposal of marriage. And shall deliberate further on my response, with your kind permission.'

I groaned. 'I don't know why I want to marry you, anyway!' Ellen, unperturbed, licked her fork daintily. And that's when I saw the cafeteria cashier waving to me and holding up her telephone receiver. I went over to her counter, took the telephone from her, and said into it, 'Hal Johnson here.'

The voice of our switchboard girl murmured into my ear, 'You about finished lunch, Hal?'

'Yeah. Why?'

'Two men here to see you. Jerry Coatsworth from the University Library and another one. A cute one.'

'Send them to my office and tell them I'll be up in a few minutes. Jerry knows where my office is.' Jerry Coatsworth, the assistant librarian at our biggest local university, bowls on my team at the College Club every Thursday night. We're good friends.

I went back to the table where I'd left Ellen. 'You can have the rest of my ice cream, baby,' I said generously. 'I've got another date.' I left and went upstairs to my office.

My office is a tiny cubicle behind the Library Director's spacious quarters. It contains only my desk and swivel chair, two visitors' chairs (castoffs from our Reading Room), a filing cabinet, and a patterned rug masquerading unconvincingly as a worn but genuine Sarouk.

Jerry and his 'cute' friend were

occupying the two visitors' chairs when I came in. I had to squeeze past them to reach my desk. 'Hi, Jerry,' I said, seating myself, 'you come to find out how a real man-sized library is run?'

'No way,' he replied, grinning. 'And not how to bowl a perfect score, either.' He said to the man in the other chair, 'This is Hal Johnson,' and to me, 'Shake hands with Perry Kavanaugh, Hal.'

I did so, across the desk. Kavanaugh was somewhere in his late twenties, I judged — blond, fresh-faced, with rumpled long-ish hair and a drooping mustache. He reminded me of the sun-bleached types you see riding horses in the cigarette ads. Cute, all right. He was smiling, but his eyes were anxious-looking, and he had been sitting on the edge of his chair even before he leaned forward to shake hands with me.

I sent an inquiring look at Jerry. 'What can I do for you?'

'We're in trouble, Hal,' Jerry said, 'and I promised Mr. Kavanaugh I'd ask you to help us get out of it.'

'What kind of trouble?'

'Mr. Kavanaugh,' said Jerry, 'is the executor of his Uncle Ralph's estate. His uncle died a few days ago. His uncle's will leaves a number of his books to us — to the Brightstone University Library — to form the nucleus of a collection of rare volumes for his alma mater that he hoped would ultimately bear his name. Like the Beinecke Rare Book Library at Yale. You with me so far?'

I nodded. 'The books your uncle left to the library were rare books?' I asked Kavanaugh.

'It seems so,' he replied. 'First editions and so on. I don't know a rare book from Adam's off ox myself, but Mr. Coatsworth here tells me — '

Jerry broke in, 'They're listed and described in the will, Hal; and yes, they'd qualify as rare books. Yes, indeed.'

'So where's the trouble?' I asked.

'The trouble is,' said Jerry, 'that Mr. Kavanaugh gave the books away six months ago.'

Kavanaugh flushed in embarrassment. 'Before I *knew* they were rare books,' he hastened to defend himself. 'And before I knew they were to be a legacy to Mr. Coatsworth's library.'

Already guessing the answer, I asked, 'Who'd you give them to, Mr. Kavanaugh?'

'To you,' Kavanaugh said. 'To the Public Library.'

'And you want them back?'

'Yes. So I can carry out the provisions of my uncle's will.'

Jerry added inelegantly, 'And *we* want those books so bad we can taste them!'

I sat back in my chair. 'How'd you happen to give them to us, Mr. Kavanaugh?'

He seemed glad of the chance to explain. 'My uncle was an old man living here alone in a rented apartment since his retirement. He's been ailing for years, nothing too serious until six months ago when his friends and neighbors and doctor began to worry about his deteriorating health and frequent mental lapses, and his doctor decided he ought to go into a nursing home. I was Uncle Ralph's only living relative, so his doctor called me in New York to see if I'd come down here and help him make the move. So I got a leave of absence from my job and came down to do what I could to help him. I got him admitted to Cedar Manor Health Center, helped him move in, and cleaned out his old apartment. Actually, I gave away most of his belongings just to get rid of them.'

'Including his books?'

'Right. Seven big cartons of them. I offered them to you — the Public Library — and you seemed happy to take them off my hands.' Kavanaugh smoothed his rumpled hair with one hand. 'It was only after my uncle's death two days ago, when I came down to make the funeral arrangements, that I discovered I had inadvertently given you the rare books he wanted the Brightstone Library to have.'

'Didn't you know he owned some rare books?' I asked. 'Hadn't he ever mentioned them to you or told you he was a collector?'

'Never.'

'Not even when he knew you were going to clear out his old apartment?'

Kavanaugh shook his head. 'He was suffering from advanced arteriosclerosis,

163

Mr. Johnson. He wasn't even aware he was living in a new place when he entered the nursing home. He didn't remember much of anything about himself or his past or — or me, for that matter. So I just went ahead on my own and did what I figured ought to be done — cleared out his apartment, terminated his lease, arranged with his bank to take care of his expenses, and so on.'

Jerry said, 'He gave you the books by mistake, Hal. So, what do you think? Is there a chance you still have them?'

'Maybe fifty-fifty,' I said. 'Depends on what they were and what shape they were in when we got them. Any donated books we can't use, we usually sell off at periodic book sales.' I turned to Mr. Kavanaugh. 'Did we give you a receipt for the books when you donated them?'

'Yes, and at least I was smart enough to save that!' Kavanaugh got it out of his pocket and handed it to me. It was one of our regular receipt forms which merely acknowledged a donation of 193 hard-cover and 55 paperback books to the Public Library by Ralph Kavanaugh of the Crest View Apartments. No book titles or anything specific. The receipt was dated the twentieth of the previous October, and signed by Mary Cutler, our chief librarian.

'Okay,' I said. 'May I keep this temporarily?' Kavanaugh nodded. 'And I'll need a list of titles — the rare book ones — to check on. The ones mentioned in the will.'

Kavanaugh handed me a typed list. 'We came prepared,' he said. 'There are only six.'

The list read:

Ulysses by James Joyce. 1922

The Adventures of Huckleberry Finn by Mark Twain. 1884

Psalterium Americanum by Cotton Mather. 1718 (Autographed)

The Sun Also Rises by Ernest Hemingway. 1926

For Whom the Bell Tolls by Ernest Hemingway. 1940

Tamerlane and Other Poems by A Bostonian. 1827

'Are these the publication dates?' I asked.

'Yes,' Jerry said.

'Okay.' I stood up. 'That's it for now, then. I'll check and let you know how I make out. I can't promise anything, of course. But I'll give it a whirl.'

'We sure appreciate it, Hal,' said Jerry. 'Thanks a million.'

Kavanaugh added his thanks to Jerry's.

I waved a deprecatory hand. 'I'll be in touch,' I said, and they left.

Ten minutes later I had given the whole story to Dr. Forbes, our Director. He listened in silence. At the end of my recital, he said, 'If we've still got the books, Hal, we'll have to return them to Mr. Kavanaugh. Legally, they're the rightful property of the Brightstone University Library.'

'They must be worth a bundle,' I ventured, 'if they're really rare books, Dr. Forbes. We could be giving up a potential fortune, couldn't we?'

He smiled. 'Yes, but it's a fortune to which the library has no reasonable claim, I'm afraid. Since the books are in our possession — if they still are — only because of a misunderstanding, we must return them to their proper owner. I suggest you consult Mrs. Cutler to see if we still have them.'

Mary Cutler, our chief librarian, listened to my story — not in silence, like Dr. Forbes, but with frequent interjections of dismay, regret, and indignation. Books are a passion with her — all books, whether rare or common or neither; she loves and treasures them, and she disliked intensely the idea that her dear Public Library might have to relinquish any of the precious volumes on our shelves to that 'stuck-up' University Library across town.

However, she promised to look into the matter at once. And with the aid of our computer, and that of the assistant librarians who are normally charged with sorting, cataloguing, and preparing donated books for circulation or sale, it didn't take her long. By the following afternoon I was ready to report to Mr. Kavanaugh and Jerry Coatsworth.

Their eyes went instantly to the small stack of books on my desk as they settled themselves into my visitors' chairs.

'Hey!' cried Jerry exuberantly. 'You found them, Hal!'

'Thank God!' was Kavanaugh's devout comment.

I said, 'Some of them, Jerry. I found five out of six.'

That calmed them down a little. But Kavanaugh exclaimed, 'Five out of six is wonderful, Mr. Johnson! Just great, and in only one day! Doesn't that mean you may still find the sixth?'

I shook my head. 'I'm afraid not. We have no record at all of the missing book, whereas these five here were simple to trace. One of the five, the *Psalterium Americanum* by Cotton Mather, had been put in our special section, where the books may be consulted with the librarian's permission here in the library, but not borrowed or taken out of the building. The other four books here were circulating as three-week books in the regular way. Both the Hemingways had been checked out, and I had to collect them from the borrowers this morning.'

Kavanaugh said anxiously, 'What about

the missing one, Mr. Johnson? The one you couldn't trace?'

'It must have been sold at one of our used-book sales. That's all we can figure — that the sorter who went through your uncle's cartons of books decided it was too fragile, or old, or unpopular or something, to be of any use to us. It probably went for a buck or two to some member of our reading public. As I say, we don't have any record of it, and we don't have it among our uncatalogued books. We looked.'

Jerry groaned. 'A buck or two!'

Kavanaugh said, 'I was a complete damn fool!'

'Anyway,' I said, patting the books at my elbow, 'our records show these are five of the six rare books you gave us by mistake. I'll need a receipt from you, Mr. Kavanaugh, stating that we have returned them to you.' I shoved the books over to him.

'Wait a minute!' Jerry said. 'Which book didn't you find? Which one is missing?'

I consulted their list. 'This *Tamerlane* thing by A Bostonian,' I said.

Jerry groaned again. 'Wouldn't you know? This *Tamerlane* 'thing,' as you call it, is the most valuable book of the whole lot! I was planning to make it the centerpiece of our new rare-book collection!' He looked deeply distressed.

I stared at him. So did Mr. Kavanaugh. 'What's so special about *Tamerlane*?'

Jerry said, 'Only that in 1827 when it was published, a certain famous American writer wasn't well enough known yet to get his name on a book, so he used that pseudonym, 'A Bostonian' instead. You know who 'A Bostonian' really was?'

'Who?' asked Kavanaugh and I together.

'Edgar Allan Poe,' said Jerry in a dismal voice. 'The last time one of these *Tamerlane* 'things' was auctioned off, you know how much it fetched?'

'How much?' said Kavanaugh and I, again as one voice.

'A hundred and forty thousand dollars.'

Nobody said anything for a minute. Kavanaugh and I were too shocked, and Jerry was too depressed. I pointed to the five books on my desk. 'How about these?'

Jerry spread his hands in a belittling gesture. 'They're rare books, and they're worth a good deal, of course. But peanuts compared to *Tamerlane*. The Cotton Mather, with his signature on the flyleaf, and the Mark Twain, might go at auction for five thousand apiece. The two Hemingways at maybe two thousand apiece. Ditto for the *Ulysses*.' He paused. 'Do you think there's *any* chance of recovering the missing book, Hal?'

'We'll give it another try, but I can't hold out too much hope.'

Jerry stared gloomily at his feet. Finally, he lifted his head. 'Anyway, Hal, it's no skin off your nose. You've been great to get these five back, and we appreciate it. Mr. Kavanaugh, how about giving Hal his receipt?'

I pushed a form over to Kavanaugh, already filled out and requiring only his signature. While he was groping in his pocket for a pen, I said to Jerry, 'I didn't know you were a rare-book buff.'

'I'm not. I read up on the six books after we were informed of the contents of the will.'

I said, 'I can see why the Cotton Mather, with his signature on it, would be a rare book. But what about these others?'

Jerry managed a grin. He took the copy of *The Adventures of Huckleberry Finn* out of the pile and leafed through the book for a minute, then put it down on the desk in front of me, opened to an illustration of an old man. 'Look at that fellow,' he said.

I looked. Then I did a double-take and looked again. 'His fly's open!'

'Right. In this 1884 edition, a disgruntled pressman altered the engraving of the illustration so that this guy's fly was open instead of closed. They call this the 'open-fly copy,' and it's worth much more than a correct copy of the edition would be.'

I laughed. Kavanaugh said, 'You're joking!'

'No, I'm not. The *Ulysses* is a first edition, published in 1922, but the Hemingways are a little unusual.' He leafed through the copy of *The Sun Also Rises*. Then, like a proud child playing

Show and Tell at kindergarten, he placed the open book in front of Kavanaugh and pointed. 'Page 181,' he said. 'Do you see that word 'stopped'?'

'Yes,' Kavanaugh said. 'What's rare about that?'

'How is it spelled?'

Kavanaugh looked again. 'With three p's!'

Jerry nodded. 'Part of the first run had that misspelling before it was caught and corrected. So this uncorrected copy is considered by rare-book buffs to be the genuine first edition.' He held up *For Whom the Bell Tolls*. 'This is a first edition, 1940. For most of the first run of this one, the photographic credit line under Hemingway's picture on the back of the dust jacket was mistakenly omitted. See? Like this copy. Consequently this is more valuable than the corrected first-edition copies with dust jackets.'

'Well, well,' I said. 'You learn something new every day, don't you?'

Kavanaugh handed me my receipt. 'What do we do next?' he asked helplessly.

'Get together with your lawyer,' I suggested.

'We tried to,' Jerry said, 'but he's in Washington at a meeting of the Bar Association. Back Monday.'

'You need him,' I said to Kavanaugh. 'You need him bad. For what you've done by giving those books to us was to dissipate some of the valuable assets of your uncle's estate, of which you are the executor. That's a real no-no to the legal boys. Your lawyer will have to figure out a way to persuade the probate court to accept your uncle's will for probate in spite of the missing assets.'

'Can he do it?' Kavanaugh was suddenly downcast.

'I don't know. The receipt we gave you when you donated the books may help. Your recovery of these five books here will be reasonable proof that you gave the rare books to us by mistake. You will probably need an affidavit from us stating that we unknowingly sold the missing book at public sale to an unknown buyer. And you'll certainly have to advertise for the missing book, offering a reward, as reasonable proof that you made all possible efforts to get it back for the legatee.'

Jerry wagged his head. 'What are you, Hal?' he asked. 'A lawyer as well as a cop?'

'No. But I'm surrounded by about a million reference books here.'

Kavanaugh sat up and said, with more enthusiasm now, 'I'll place the ads this afternoon, Mr. Johnson. How much reward shall I offer?'

'Don't name an amount. Just say 'generous reward.' And don't mention 'rare book,' for God's sake. You just want to get the book back for sentimental reasons.'

'Okay,' Kavanaugh said. He stood up and Jerry followed suit. 'And thanks for your help, Mr. Johnson. I don't know what we'd have done without you.'

He gathered up his five books and they left, trailing expressions of gratitude as they went.

★ ★ ★

That was Wednesday. I waited until Friday evening before I called the telephone number listed in Mr. Kavanaugh's advertisements.

I draped a handkerchief over the mouthpiece of my telephone.

When he answered, I said through the handkerchief, in as hoarse a voice as I could manage, 'Are you the one who's been advertising for a book?'

'Why, yes,' said Kavanaugh promptly. '*Tamerlane and Other Poems*. Why do you ask?'

'I've got it,' I said.

A sharp intake of breath and a long moment of silence at the other end of the line told me all I wanted to know. I went on, 'How much is the reward?'

Kavanaugh said, 'Are you sure you have the book I advertised for?'

'Yep,' I said. 'So how much is the reward?'

A hesitation. Then Kavanaugh said, 'Do you mind telling me who you are? And how you happen to have the book?'

'Never mind that until we get the reward settled. Books are the way I make my living, and I just got lucky when I spotted the one you want.'

'Lucky?' Kavanaugh sounded thoroughly bewildered.

'Yeah. The book's worth a lot of money, isn't it? So the reward should be pretty big, shouldn't it?'

'I — hadn't settled on a specific amount. You'll get whatever seems fair, of course.'

'How about ten thousand dollars?' I said. 'The *Tamerlane* thing is worth that much reward, isn't it?'

'Well, that's pretty steep, don't you think? The book has only a sentimental value to me.'

'How about if we talk it over before you decide? Are you free now?'

'Yes, but — '

'Great. Come over to my place. You can make sure my book is the one you want. And we can bargain a little about the reward. I live in apartment twelve at Pennfield Gardens.'

'Where's that?' asked Kavanaugh. 'I'm pretty much a stranger in town.'

'Your cabbie will know the way. I'll look for you in about twenty minutes.'

Actually, he made it in seventeen, which is pretty good going. At his knock, I opened the front door without turning on the light in the vestibule, so he was inside before he got a good look at my face.

Then he stood stock-still and stared. 'Mr. Johnson!' he exclaimed. 'Was it *you* who telephoned me about the missing book?'

'Yeah,' I said. 'Come on in and sit down where we can talk this whole thing over.'

He advanced into my living room and, dazed, sat down stiffly in an armchair with his back to my bedroom door. I sat opposite him on the sofa.

'I don't understand this at all, Mr. Johnson. Why did you call me and pretend to have found my book?'

'Because,' I said quietly, 'I decided you are a rank amateur and need some professional help.'

'Such as yours?'

'Exactly. Such as mine.'

'What professional help can you offer

me, for God's sake?' asked Kavanaugh, a little wildly.

'I can tell you where your missing book is, for starters.'

Kavanaugh blinked. 'Where?'

'In New York. Either in your safety-deposit box, or squirreled away in your home.'

He drew a deep breath and ran a hand over his blond hair. 'Now I think I understand,' he said. 'You're trying to blackmail me, aren't you, Mr. Johnson?'

'Call me Hal,' I said. 'And let's not talk about blackmail. I'd rather consider it a reward for locating your missing book. I think about half of what you could get for it at auction would be a fair reward. Say, roughly seventy thousand dollars, if we can trust Jerry Coatsworth's figure.'

He said, matter-of-factly, 'It probably won't bring that much. Anyway, what makes you think I'll split with you? You can't prove anything against me. I can destroy the book, then it would be merely your word against mine. And whose word do you think the probate court would take?'

I slid in the clincher very gently. 'They'd take mine,' I said, 'unless you had that affidavit from the Public Library that I mentioned to you.'

That stopped him for a few seconds. Then, 'My lawyer could get around that, Johnson, and you know it as well as I do.' But his voice held uncertainty.

'You're dreaming. Your goose is cooked, Kavanaugh, unless you agree to cooperate with me.'

'Well . . . ' He hesitated. Then he sketched a tight smile. 'Do you mind telling me how I gave myself away? Why you think me such an amateur?'

I ticked the points off on my fingers. 'First, I found it slightly odd — and thought-provoking — that the only book we couldn't locate was the most valuable one. Second, I didn't believe for a minute that you never knew your uncle owned rare books or had willed them to the Brightstone Library. It seemed much more likely that as his appointed executor under his will, you'd been given a copy of the will long ago, with the rare books listed in it. And third, I couldn't quite accept the presumed fact that our people, who sorted your uncle's books, would be dumb enough to discard a book like *Tamerlane* without first checking with our chief librarian.'

Kavanaugh said nothing. His expression, by rights, should have been sheepish after my little lecture. Instead, he looked thoughtful. I asked him, 'Why did you decide to steal your uncle's books anyway? As his only living relative, you're probably the heir to everything he had *except* the books, aren't you?'

He nodded. 'Yes. But I knew when I moved him into that nursing home that if he lived for more than a year at those prices, he wouldn't have a nickel left to his name except his Social Security. So I was merely trying to salvage a little bit of his estate for myself before it was too late.'

I said, 'Well, you had a good idea, Kavanaugh, but you handled it like an amateur.' I grinned at him. 'Which is where I come in.'

With the air of a man asking a very important question, Kavanaugh said,

'How many other people have you told about this?'

I gave him my you-must-be-out-of-your-head look. 'Cut anybody else in on this sweet little setup? The only chance to get in on some big money I'll ever have? I haven't breathed it to another soul. I'm telling you the truth.'

'Good,' Kavanaugh said, in what sounded like a relieved tone. He put his hand inside his jacket, pulled out a dainty little automatic, and pointed it at me.

I was dumbfounded.

Kavanaugh stood up, took two paces toward me, and directed the round cold eye of his gun at the general area of my midsection. No doubt aiming, I thought, to slaughter some of the butterflies that had suddenly come alive there.

I swallowed hard, like taking a big pill without water. 'Hey!' I got out in a squeak. 'Hold it!'

Kavanaugh's gun hand was trembling, I saw, but not enough to make much difference to me if he pulled the trigger. He said, with a thread of smugness in his voice, 'I knew it was you who telephoned me tonight. So I brought this with me in case you got any big ideas.' He waggled the gun, and sweat broke out on my normally placid brow.

'You knew it was me on the phone?'

'Of course. You're not as professional as you seem to think, Johnson.' He was thoroughly enjoying my discomfiture.

'How did you know it was me?'

'Because you referred to the *Tamerlane* book as the *Tamerlane* 'thing,' just as you did in your office when you discussed it with Coatsworth and me.'

I winced. He had a point. An amateur he might be, but he was not a complete fool. I said. 'You figure to shoot me? In cold blood? Right now?'

'Why not? Without you around to interfere with my handling of the *Tamerlane* 'thing,' my little scheme could still work.'

I looked down at the gun menacing my stomach and said, 'If I were you, Kavanaugh, I wouldn't shoot me.' I fed him the old cliché. 'You'd never get away with it.'

He said tauntingly, towering over me,

'Why not, Mr. Professional?'

I looked over his shoulder toward my bedroom and said loudly, 'Come on in, Jerry. Did you hear it all?'

Startled, Kavanaugh took his eyes off me long enough for me to twist the gun out of his hand, after which I thrust it, none too gently, into *his* stomach.

He gasped.

I said, 'You *are* an amateur, Kavanaugh. That looking-over-the-shoulder trick is as old as the hills. And I see you even forgot to take the safety off your gun. Now, sit down and listen to me.' I emphasized my request with another stiff prod of the gun barrel.

Slowly, he backed up and sagged into his chair.

'I deliberately rigged this whole affair tonight,' I informed him. 'And you're now tied up so tight you better stop squirming or you'll really get hurt.'

Kavanaugh said sullenly, 'You rigged it?'

I nodded. 'I've got our entire conversation on tape. How does that grab you?'

His eyes widened. He lifted his gaze

from the gun in my hand to my face.

He didn't say anything, however, so I went on quickly, 'I don't intend to use the tape against you — even though the police, your lawyer, the probate judge, and the Brightstone University Library would find it very interesting indeed.'

'Why did you tape it then?' he asked.

'An anchor to windward,' I answered, 'in case you refuse to cooperate.'

'I don't believe you taped anything.'

'The mike's under the arm of your chair.' He ran his fingers along the underside of his chair arm and found the mike. He still didn't say anything, just sank a little deeper into his chair. I allowed him a silent minute to think things over.

At length he said, 'Cooperate. What the hell do you mean, cooperate?' He frowned, the sullen look replaced now by a contemplative one. 'What do you want from me, Johnson?'

'The book,' I said. 'The *Tamerlane*.'

'Half the loot isn't enough for you? You want it all, is that it?'

'Who are you to complain?' I said.

'After all, you just tried to kill me to hang on to the whole bundle for yourself.' I shook the clip out of his automatic and tossed the empty gun into his lap across the few feet separating us. I said, 'What I want you to do is to give the book to the Brightstone Library, just as directed in your uncle's will.'

That wiped the contemplative look off his face and replaced it with one that was half-puzzled, half-astonished, and wholly ludicrous. It was all I could do to keep from laughing.

'You're not going to sell the book at auction?'

'No way, buster,' I said firmly.

'Then what's in it for you?'

'Look,' I said. 'Jerry Coatsworth is going to be in charge of the Brightstone new rare-book collection. And Jerry Coatsworth is a friend of mine. I'm not going to stand around and see him cheated out of his rare books by an amateur crook who doesn't know any more about stealing than I do about playing left field for the Cubs. Especially when you try to make *my* library the fall guy in the sketch. Does that answer your question?'

He had the grace to look embarrassed. 'Yeah,' he murmured. 'I guess so.'

'So here's what I want you to do. Get the book from wherever you've hidden it. Tell your lawyer and Jerry Coatsworth that some guy who bought it at a local used-book sale saw your ad in the papers and returned it to you for the reward.'

'I can't just say 'some guy',' protested Kavanaugh. 'And how much reward?'

'How about five hundred dollars? Could you scrape up that much? Not from your uncle's estate, but from your own funds?'

'Sure.'

'Okay. Then you write a check for five hundred bucks to the Public Library Building Fund. We're opening a new branch on the South Side. And you tell Coatsworth and your lawyer and the probate court that the guy who returned the book wanted to remain anonymous, and asked you to give his reward to the Public Library. You got it?'

Kavanaugh began to perk up. 'Sure, I

got it, Hal. And if I do it that way, you'll never say anything about what really happened? You'll never — ah — ?'

'Never breathe a word?' I gave him my biggest trustworthy grin. 'You'll have to hope so, won't you?'

Kavanaugh got out of his chair, put his little gun away, and held out a hand to me. 'It's a deal,' he promised solemnly. Then he added impulsively, 'And a better one than I deserve, Hal. Thank you for making me keep my amateur status.'

That night, I took Ellen out for dinner, made her swear a sacred oath of secrecy, and told her the whole story. 'So you see, Ellen,' I finished up, 'I'm not only nice-looking but I'm intrepid in the face of danger, loyal to our library, and compassionate to amateurs. Don't you think you should make up your mind to marry me?'

Ellen put down her knife and fork. After a minute she said, 'Since you're such a paragon, Hal, I think I ought to confer an honorary degree on you.'

'An honorary degree would be nice,' I said, pleased. 'What degree did you have in mind?'

Ellen dimpled. 'How about B.L.S. — Bachelor of Library Science?'

'Bachelor?' I said, regarding her sorrowfully. 'You're turning me down again, aren't you? For the eighteenth time.'

'Nineteenth,' said Ellen. But she reached across the table and squeezed my hand hard, which I took for a hopeful sign.

7

Hero With a Headache

When I began to come out of it, the first things I noticed were a whirling sensation in my head with an undercurrent of thumping pain, and a very sick feeling in the pit of my stomach.

I knew I ought to open my eyes, but it didn't seem worth the trouble. So I kept them shut and went on feeling dizzy and nauseated until, vaguely, I realized that my whirling, aching head and the nausea were familiar symptoms ... something I'd gone through before, or thought I had. A kind of *déja vù* feeling, as Liz, on the library's check-out desk, would express it. She always used egghead terms like that. Or was it Kathy on the main desk? Anyway, I knew damn well I'd felt this way before. Then I pinned it down — or thought I did.

I'd been sapped. Just as I was once,

long ago, when I was working under Lieutenant Randall at the police department. Sapped by an expert. I'd felt exactly this way then.

My head went on aching, but my stomach began to settle back out of my throat. I forced myself to open my eyes, which wasn't so tough to do after all. They came open with no more than an extra stab of pain as the light hit them . . .

And there was Mrs. Miles, across the room from me, tied to a chair with a twisted pink sheet.

Then I *knew* I'd been sapped. Seeing Mrs. Miles brought it back to me almost whole. She was watching me, big-eyed and weeping, silently pleading with me to do something.

But what did she want me to do? I wasn't in too good shape to do it, whatever it was, because *I* was tied to a chair, too. My hands were fastened behind the chair back so tightly that my shoulder sockets screamed at the strain. Not with a sheet, though. This felt like clothesline. It went several times around my thighs, waist and chest, and fastened me to the chair tight as a politician's schedule.

We were in a den or study or office. It was a medium-large room with a desk and telephone, two deep leather chairs, the two straight chairs that held Mrs. Miles and me, wall-to-wall aqua carpeting, drapes of the same color, and a whole wall of books. In a home like Mrs. Miles', I guess you'd call it a library. Mrs. Miles was tied to the desk chair. My chair was across the room from hers in a corner near the bookshelves.

I licked my lips and was considerably pleased that I could, for that meant my mouth wasn't pasted shut with a strip of adhesive tape like Mrs. Miles'. I figured fuzzily that therefore I ought to be able to talk, so I tried it. My words came out, 'Wheewhis Whow,' thick and hoarse, instead of 'Mrs. Miles' as I had intended.

By this time, my head had slowed its spinning enough so that I could think a little more clearly. All that got me was a feeling of guilt and embarrassment at how stupid I'd been to get into this mess in the first place. I'd made a fool of myself

— and of poor Mrs. Miles too, for that matter. And nobody to blame but myself. Old Hal Johnson, a trained police officer, acting like any callow Sir Galahad, for God's sake.

Not that I was actually a cop anymore, but I'd *been* one. Come to think of it, maybe that accounted for my sticking my nose into Mrs. Miles' business instead of minding my own. My own business nowadays, let me explain, was simply chasing down overdue and stolen books for the public library. I was still fuzz in a way, I suppose, but sissy fuzz. Library fuzz, for Pete's sake.

The first name on my list of overdue library book-borrowers that morning had been Mrs. J. Miles, 1525 Washburn Drive, on the West Side. I like to start my day out with a little class as much as anyone, so I was glad the address was in a good neighborhood. The houses were mostly split-levels and spacious, set well back from the street with a lot of manicured lawn around them.

There are a lot of reasons — and I've heard them all, believe me — why people who borrow books from the public library fail to return them on time, and then ignore the overdue notices the library sends out to them as reminders. One reason is that the book borrower is just too lazy to bother bringing the books back and too rich to give a damn about the fines he'll have to pay as a result. 1525 Washburn looked like one of that kind to me. Lazy and rich.

It was ten minutes to nine when I pulled up there, parked behind a dark green van that said 'Heritage Cleaners' on the sides in sloppy lettering, and walked up the long flagstone path to the front door. On the way, I admired the Indiana limestone facing of the house and the gleaming Thunderbird standing on the left side of the open two-car garage.

I rang the doorbell, only it wasn't a bell, it was chimes. I could hear them sending musical notes through the house to announce my arrival. Nothing happened, so after a minute or so, I gave the chimes another thumbing and waited some more. This time, sounds of movement inside the door told me that somebody was at home after all. I could hear a chain rattling, then a bolt being turned, and then the door was drawn open and a handsome middle-aged woman with gray hair and dimples was looking at me inquiringly.

'Mrs. Miles?' I asked.

She nodded, but didn't say anything, although I could see her swallow as if she was getting ready to. I went into my usual spiel. 'I'm from the public library,' I said, showing her my identification card, 'and I've come about all those overdue books you have.'

She looked at my identification card suspiciously. Then she cleared her throat and said, 'Oh — oh, yes. Those would be the books I took out of the library to amuse my grandson when he was visiting us last month.' She cleared her throat again. 'I — I'll return them as soon as — as I can, Mr. Johnson.'

I said, 'I'll take them off your hands right now and save you the trip.'

'Oh . . . well, thank you,' she said ungraciously. 'Wait there a minute, then.' She pushed the door to and went away.

She didn't ask me in. Lazy and rich, all right, I thought, and not very polite, either.

I cooled my heels for a couple of minutes before she came back with an armload of children's picture books. 'Here,' she said in a harassed voice and thrust them at me. She was angry and distraught and I got the feeling that she thought I ought to apologize to her for bothering her so early in the morning. She was obviously anxious to get rid of me and no two ways about it.

As she was about to close the door in my face, therefore, I took a little malicious pleasure in saying, 'Wait, Mrs. Miles. You owe a fine on these books. They're way overdue, you know.'

She gave me a strange look. 'A — a fine? Oh, *dear*! How much?'

I told her the fine came to six dollars and thirty cents.

'Well — all right. W-wait till I get my purse,' she stammered in what suddenly seemed like distress. She went away again.

When she returned, she handed me the

exact amount of the fine, and I said, 'Thank you, Mrs. Miles. You know, you can renew library books and avoid the fine.'

As I turned to leave, to my great surprise she suddenly reached out a hand and touched my arm lightly. I turned back to her. She pointed to the top book of the pile I was carrying. 'My grandson thought this one was particularly good,' she said in a hushed murmur, and tapped her forefinger twice on the title: *The Robber of Featherbed Lane*. Both taps landed lightly on the word *Robber*. Her hand was shaking.

I went out to the street, deposited her books in the back seat of my car, and climbed behind the wheel, vaguely troubled about Mrs. Miles. Old police habits of thought don't die easily. I couldn't help thinking that, if I were still a real cop, I'd be curious about the answers to several questions that occurred to me in connection with my visit to Mrs. Miles.

Question one — why was Mrs. Miles, normally a pleasant and lighthearted woman if her dimples and smile lines meant anything, so disagreeable, impolite — and, yes, agitated — over my simple demand for a batch of overdue library books?

Question two — how come Mrs. Miles stammered noticeably sometimes and didn't stammer other times?

Question three — where was the driver of the Heritage Cleaners van that was still parked ahead of my car?

Question four — why did Mrs. Miles delay my departure at the last minute with a trite remark about her grandson when, up to then, she'd been trying like crazy to get rid of me?

Finally, question five — how about that trembling finger tapping the word *Robber* so pointedly?

To tell you the truth, I didn't have the guts to drive away from Mrs. Miles' house leaving these questions unanswered behind me. I knew I'd feel like an all-American heel later on if I did. I've always been a sucker for women in distress, anyway. That's one reason why I'm not with the police department any longer.

So, I thought, *let's see if Mrs. Miles is really caught in a pickle.*

I looked up Heritage Cleaners in the telephone book and the city directory — both of which I carry in my car to check addresses when I'm on the job — and you know what? There was no firm called Heritage Cleaners listed in either one. Yet not more than four feet ahead of my car's front bumper sat a dark-green van with 'Heritage Cleaners' lettered on the sides, big as life.

What would you think? What would anybody think? The same thing I thought, I'm sure. Except that what you'd do about it would probably be much more sensible than what I did about it. You'd call the cops. But I used to *be* a cop, so I thought I could handle Mrs. Miles' trouble by myself.

I crawled out of my car and went up the flagstone walk to the front door again, then rang the chimes. In due course, the door was opened again. This time, though, it wasn't Mrs. Miles who faced me. It was a smooth-faced man of indeterminate age with a black mustache, long sideburns, and hair cut as short as my own.

I said, 'Mrs. Miles, you didn't give me back — *oh*, you're not Mrs. Miles, are you?'

'No,' he said. 'I'm Mr. Miles. Can I help you?'

'Well, I'm from the public library, Mr. Miles, and a few minutes ago, when I collected some overdue library books from your wife, she must've missed one. She paid the fines on all of them, but I checked the titles and she still has one book.'

'Which book is that?' He raised an eyebrow.

I said the first thing that came into my mind. 'A picture book called *Cato the Kiwi Bird*.'

He nodded. 'It's possible my wife still has it. But she's very busy right now. So come back some other time, okay?' He began to shut the door.

I lowered my right shoulder and charged the door with it like a defensive tackle on the blitz. I thought I could use the door as a battering ram to throw him off-balance enough, even if he had a gun

— as seemed likely — to give me time in the confusion to get inside the house where I could handle him.

But no. A split second before my shoulder hit the closing door, he suddenly reversed his stance and pulled the door wide open instead of slamming it shut. The result was that, failing to encounter the expected resistance to my lunge, I catapulted through the opening, tripped on the doorsill, and went down full-length on my face inside the entrance hall.

Then Mr. Miles closed the door. I heard it slam. I twisted my head around and caught a brief glimpse of a snub-nosed automatic in Mr. Miles' left hand. He stooped over me and ground the barrel of the gun painfully into my back at about the place where I imagine my right kidney is.

'What was that book again, friend?' he asked in an expressionless voice.

'*Cato the Kiwi Bird*,' I repeated, feeling like a fool but also knowing that one little move now without his permission could get me killed.

'It sounds fascinating,' he said. 'I'll

have to read it sometime.'

I heard a swishing sound. Then my head exploded in a big burst of orange fireworks.

★ ★ ★

The fireworks were still flashing faintly now as I looked across the library at poor Mrs. Miles, gagged with adhesive tape and tied in her chair with a pink sheet. I tried my voice again, and this time it came out much better.

'Mrs. Miles . . . '

She widened her eyes. There was still terror in them.

'He wasn't your husband, was he?' I said next. A dumb question.

She shook her head vigorously.

'I'm sorry,' I said, struggling against the clothesline on my wrists. 'He was too cute for me. Did he hurt you?'

She shook her head again. Tears were rolling down her cheeks.

'Good. Have I been out long?' My headache was making my thoughts hazy and muddled.

This time Mrs. Miles accompanied her headshake with a frantic cross-eyed look down her nose toward the mouth-sealing tape below it. Only then did it occur to me that the conversation was going to remain pretty one-sided unless I could somehow arrange for her to join in.

I gave up on my wrists and tried wriggling my feet. They were tied together with more clothesline. Not crossed, and not tied to the chair — but tied together so tightly that I hardly knew they were mine. I was relieved, all the same. Maybe the guy who sapped me wasn't such an expert after all. No tape on my mouth, ankles not crossed, and not even fastened back under the chair seat to keep my feet off the ground. Amateur stuff.

I leaned forward, my weight tipping my chair onto its front legs, my bound feet the third leg of a tripod that made it easy for me to stay balanced that way. Then I straightened my legs, put my full weight on my feet, and began to hop very carefully, a few inches per hop, toward Mrs. Miles. I was hunched over like an arthritic dwarf — I had an antique ladder-back chair strapped to my back and legs — but my feet were on the floor, and I was capable of locomotion of a sort. That was the important thing.

Reaching Mrs. Miles' chair, I paused and bent toward her face as though I was going to kiss her on the cheek. Instead, I nipped a corner of her adhesive tape between my teeth and ripped off her gag — far enough, anyway, so her mouth was uncovered. She winced and moaned as the tape came unstuck — all the same, she pulled her head back hard to help me dislodge the tape more easily.

The first sound that came out of her was a sob. The second was a name. '*Jamie!*'

'Who's Jamie?' I said.

Still crying, she worked her mouth painfully. 'My husband!' she moaned then. 'They took him away!' Her sobs came faster.

'They?' I said.

'Three of them. They had guns! Oh, Jamie . . . ' She could hardly get the words out.

'I saw one of the guns,' I remembered.

'You said *three* men?'

She wailed, 'And it's my fault they hurt *you*, too! That man untied me and made me answer the door when you rang. He told me to get rid of you if I didn't want to get shot. He — he pointed his gun at me all the time I was giving you those library books!'

'Forget it,' I said. 'You were brave to warn me the way you did. I was the dumb one.' I tried to make my headache go away by shaking my head. That made it worse. 'Two men took your husband and left one man here with you, the one who slugged me? Is that it?'

She nodded. 'The one who hit you left ten minutes ago.' Her eyes went to an electric clock on the desk to confirm that. 'The telephone rang while he was tying you up, and he answered it, and then he left right away.'

That explained my amateur tying job — he hadn't waited to finish. 'What did he say on the telephone — could you hear?'

'He said 'Okay,' that's all.'

I began to see the pattern. 'What time

was it when they took your husband away?'

'We were still at breakfast — about ten minutes after eight, I guess.' She closed her eyes and shivered uncontrollably.

'In your husband's car?' I asked, remembering the empty spot in the garage beside the Thunderbird.

She didn't seem to hear me. She started to squirm around frantically in her chair, trying to shed the twisted sheet that bound her, and moaning like a wounded animal.

I tried again. 'Mrs. Miles, where does your husband work?'

She sobbed convulsively, her mouth making ugly moues in her tear-streaked face. Her dimples made her look worse, somehow. The strip of adhesive tape was still dangling from one cheek and her eyes were wild. Hysteria was catching up with her.

I shouted to get through to her. 'Mrs. *Miles! Listen* to me! Where does your husband work? *Work!* Tell me! Don't you want to save your husband?'

She stopped squirming as suddenly as though turned to stone. The wildness went out of her eyes. 'He's the cashier of the Second Fidelity Bank,' she said in a dead voice.

'Thanks,' I said. I hopped three hops to the other side of the desk, where the telephone was, and set my chair down again on all four legs. Then I stretched forward as far as I could and flipped the telephone receiver off its stand by coming down hard on one end of it with my chin. It was a touch-type phone. The receiver fell face-up on the desk, with the dialing buttons right there under my nose.

I took this as a good omen and dialed the police emergency number with it — my nose, I mean. I had to stop and wait, after each jab at a button, to give the receiver time to stop rocking on its spine, but I finally got the number dialed. Then I got my left ear as close to the receiver as I could, and waited for the police to answer.

When they did, I raised my voice in an official bellow and yelled, '*Emergency! Get me Lieutenant Randall!*' The cop on the board must have thought I was a captain, at the least, because Randall was on the wire in almost exactly nothing flat.

'Lieutenant,' I said, 'this is Hal Johnson. Don't say anything, just listen for a minute, okay? I'm pretty sure the Second Fidelity Bank was robbed about half an hour ago by two men with the unwilling help of the bank's cashier, Mr. J. Miles. He was probably forced to open the vault after the time lock was off but before the bank opened for business at nine. The cashier's wife and I were held prisoner in Miles' home, 1525 Washburn, by a third man during the heist. We're still prisoners.

'But get this — our guard left us fifteen minutes ago, immediately after getting a phone call here. He was probably going to pick up his pals and the loot somewhere near the bank downtown. He's driving a dark green Chevrolet van labeled 'Heritage Cleaners', and should be about halfway to town by now on either Murchison or Cambria Avenue. There's still time to get the van — but don't stop it until it makes the pick-up. You got all that, Lieutenant?' I drew a deep breath.

'I got it,' he said, as cool as a well-digger's shirt tail. 'Hold on, Hal. Be right back.'

He went away, presumably to start a little action. While he was gone, I sent comforting upside-down looks at Mrs. Miles, whose sobbing had now subsided to intermittent catches of breath. Four minutes ticked slowly by on the desk clock before I heard Lieutenant Randall's voice squeaking in the receiver again.

'I've got it started, Hal. We're checking on the bank and the cashier right now. Patrol car 303 has your green van in sight on Murchison. And I've got another car coming over to you.'

'Fine,' I said. 'I'll tell Mrs. Miles that help is on the way.'

★   ★   ★

That evening, Lieutenant Randall telephoned me at home. 'What happened to you,' he said, 'after my man cut you loose this morning, with everybody waiting to give you the conquering hero treatment?'

'*Hero* treatment?' I said. 'Then the bank *was* robbed?'

'Sure. I've been trying to locate you all afternoon to tell you.'

'What about the cashier, Mr. Miles? Was he hurt?'

'Not a bit. Locked in the vault with the vault guard after the thieves had cleaned out the cash. Then they just walked out of the bank like two customers when the bank opened at nine.'

'You nailed them, I hope?'

'Sure. Your green van led us right to them — and to the loot too, Hal. Don't overlook the loot. Two hundred and twelve thousand dollars. That's why the hero treatment was ready for you, boy. Mrs. Miles told us how you happened to get mixed up in the thing. So why didn't you stick around to take a bow?'

'I had a hell of a headache.'

'Too bad, too bad,' Randall said. I knew his cat-yellow eyes would be as bland and unfeeling as two egg yolks, even as he sympathized. 'The fellow who slugged you was Teddy Thurbald, incidentally. A pro. How's the headache now?'

'I still have it.'

'Then why'd you go back to work this afternoon?'

'I didn't. I came home to bed.'

He clicked his tongue. 'You always were soft-headed, Hal — especially about broads. You haven't changed.' I didn't answer that one. 'Well, you'll probably be okay by Monday. Mr. and Mrs. Miles can thank you then.'

'They'll have to do more than thank me. They owe me money.'

Randall sounded scandalized. 'You mean you want a *reward* for helping those nice people and their bank?'

'Hell, no,' I said, 'but since I took the day off today, I won't get Mrs. Stout's overdue library books back to the library until Monday. So they owe me three more days' fines.'

'They shouldn't begrudge that,' said Randall, 'since you saved the bank two hundred and twelve grand. Matter of fact, this whole thing is going to look so good on my record that I might even pay your extra fines myself. How much do they come to?'

'Eighty-one cents,' I said grouchily and hung up. My head was killing me.

8

Sideswipe

As my car struck broadside against the
low curb and, already beginning to roll,
slammed across the bridge's walkway and
crashed through the flimsy steel railing,
my most intense emotion was one of raw
anger rather than fear.

Not that I'm a particularly fearless character, or too slow of mind to recognize
instantly the imminence of my own death.
No, what caused my outrage was simply a
long-standing pet abomination of mine
— it had marked my years as a policeman
and civilian alike — for anybody, young
or old, man or woman, who drove a car
while under the influence of alcohol or
drugs and blithely played Russian roulette
with other people's lives.

I took a flashing lopsided look through
my tilted windshield at the car that had
forced me off the bridge and through the

railing. And I suspected at once that whoever was driving it was either drunk or
high or both, because the car showed no
sign of stopping. It was drawing rapidly
away at speed.

Then I was too busy for further
thought about the departing car. My own
old Ford, carrying shards of steel railing
with it, was falling rapidly, end over end,
toward the river thirty feet below. I
thanked God fervently for my seatbelt. It
held me sturdily in place, kept me
oriented enough to permit me to do the
little things that might possibly save me
from drowning — roll up my driver's
window to the top, unlock both front
doors, and pray a bit. The prayer was only
a quickie, of course, but I hoped it might
help a little. I also thought fleetingly of
Ellen Thomas, the girl on the checkout
desk at the library, whose hand I had
been vainly seeking in marriage for lo,
these many months.

Then the car hit the water with a
resounding splash and slowly, inexorably,
carried me with it beneath the surface.

I called Lieutenant Randall, my old boss at Homicide, from the hospital early the next day. 'Lieutenant,' I asked querulously, 'did you hear what happened to me yesterday?'

'Yeah, Hal, I heard.' Randall's voice was as gruff as usual. 'Somebody forced you off the Wolf Hollow Bridge, right? And you made it to shore okay. So congratulations. You should be dead.'

'I know it,' I said. 'But thanks, anyway.'

'What were you doing on Wolf Hollow Bridge, for God's sake? Nobody uses it any more except a few farmers.'

'I was going to collect some books from a farmer's wife out at Dell Corners,' I said, 'and it was a farmer who found me beside the road when I crawled out of the river, so don't knock it.'

'You always did make friends easy. What do you want from me?'

'I want that SOB who sideswiped me on the bridge and left the scene of the accident. I want to find out who's responsible for my bath. And for the total loss of my car. And for the destruction of the forty-two library books that were in the trunk when we went overboard.'

Randall said, 'You and your library books. You're a little confused, aren't you? Hit-and-run, leaving the scene, DWI — you don't want me, you want Traffic. Aside from that, how you feeling?'

'I got a knot on my head, a sprained thumb, and a cracked rib. But the doctor says I can leave here today if I promise not to breathe deep and don't go bowling for a while.'

'Great,' said Randall. 'Get lots of rest. And hold on. I'll switch you to Traffic.'

'Wait a minute! That guy could have killed me!'

'You *aren't* dead, though, are you? So it's none of my business.' There was a click in my ear and a new voice said, 'Traffic. Sergeant O'Rourke.'

I said, 'Jerry, let me talk to Lieutenant Henderson. This is Hal Johnson.' I knew Jerry from the old days.

'Hey, Hal, we heard you got dunked. You okay?'

'Yeah,' I said, 'but boiling mad. I hope

Henderson can find my H-and-R driver for me. I'd like to say a few choice words to him. Is Henderson there?'

'Hold on.'

Henderson came on the wire. 'How you doing, Hal?'

I said, 'Okay, Lieutenant. But I'm mad as hell. Will you please find out for me who the joker was who ran me off Wolf Hollow Bridge yesterday?'

'I wish I could,' said Henderson regretfully. 'There's not much chance, though, with no witnesses and nowhere to start.'

'Listen,' I said, 'I'm going to *give* you a place to start. I saw the license number of the car that knocked me off the bridge.'

'Oho!' Henderson sounded suddenly cheerful. 'Let's have it then, Hal. Maybe we can get you some raw beef for dinner after all.'

They were just gathering up the breakfast trays at the hospital when Henderson called back. 'Hal?'

'Quick work, Lieutenant. Any luck?'

'Not much. I'm sorry. The car that sideswiped you is registered to a man named Frank Shoemaker at 818 Northway Road, Apartment 3.'

'Frank Shoemaker, 818 Northway Road, Apartment 3. I got it. Thanks, Lieutenant.' I felt my anger beginning to build anew. 'Did you take him in?'

'No. Shoemaker reported his car stolen from the Haas Brothers parking lot downtown at twelve noon yesterday. Shoemaker's on the Haas security staff. Cruiser 23 found his car abandoned in the East End at six-thirty this morning. With the right side pretty well bashed in.'

'Hell's bells!' I said, seething. 'Just my luck! I'm forced off a bridge and nearly killed by a drunken thief who'll get away with it scot free — and the next time he gets high and feels like a joyride in a stolen car, he'll go right out and endanger the lives of other innocent citizens!' I tried to calm down, contain my fury.

'Look at it this way,' said Henderson. 'You're still in one piece, Hal. And that ain't bad for starters. So take it easy. I'll see you around.'

* ★ ★

They released me from the hospital about eleven o'clock. I took a taxi to the rent-a-car office nearest the library. There, I rented a Chevy Citation to get me around on my collection routes until the Ford was either dragged out of the river and repaired, or declared a total loss and replaced by the insurance company. Meanwhile, my insurance covered the rental of the Chevy, which helped. Library detectives like me, who track down stolen and overdue books for the public library, aren't the highest paid people in the world, and I needed all the money I could muster if I was ever going to set up housekeeping with Ellen Thomas.

If. She hadn't said yes yet, but I thought she was weakening a little. Why else would she have telephoned twice after she found out I was in the hospital, and sounded so pleased when I assured her I was still my usual handsome, carefree self with no arms or legs in splints and no bandages around my head?

I drove my rented car to the library, reported in to the Director, and picked up the overdue-books list from my office. Then I went about my business as usual, trying to ignore the occasional sharp pain from the cracked rib and the throbbing of the sprained thumb.

About three in the afternoon, I made a call at an apartment just around the corner from Haas Brothers Department Store, and it occurred to me that as long as I was in the neighborhood I'd go and have a little chat with Frank Shoemaker.

Leaving the Chevy — locked up tight — in the parking lot, I went into the store and asked at the information desk where I could find Shoemaker of the security staff.

The pretty blonde at the desk said, 'He's around somewhere. I saw him only a few minutes ago. Try back toward the book department. That way.' She pointed. 'Do you know him?'

'No, I don't.'

'Well, you can recognize him by his hair and mustache,' she said. 'They're almost pure white. And his skin is almost black right now, he's so tanned. He's just back from a Florida vacation.'

'Thanks,' I said. 'I'll have a look.'

I headed for the book department, keeping a sharp eye out for a man with white hair and mustache and a tan. I was only halfway there when the possible significance of the girl's words struck me. I'm sure the clerks at the nearby perfume counter must have thought I had experienced a sudden revelation of some sort, like St. Paul on the road to Damascus or something, because I stopped dead in my tracks and stood stock-still in the middle of the aisle while busy shoppers sidestepped around me.

When at length I got moving again and located Shoemaker at the jewelry counter, I inspected him carefully and decided I wouldn't speak to him after all. At least for now.

★   ★   ★

An hour later I was facing Lieutenant Randall across his cluttered desk. 'It wasn't a hit-and-run,' I said, 'and it wasn't a DWI, and it wasn't leaving the scene of an accident, Lieutenant. It was attempted murder. And that *is* your department.'

Randall kept his cat-yellow eyes on me without blinking. 'What makes you think so?'

'Mostly a hunch — with a few bits of evidence to back it up. Want to hear?'

He nodded.

'Okay. I got this sudden idea that somebody had been trying to kill me only an hour ago. I dropped into Haas Brothers to see the guy who owns the car that knocked me off the bridge yesterday.'

'Fellow named Shoemaker, right?' said Randall.

'But he wasn't driving when you were pushed,' Peterson said.

I was touched. That meant Randall had been interested enough in my welfare to follow up Traffic's investigation. I said, 'What started me thinking was that Shoemaker has a heavy Florida tan.'

Randall gave me a kind of look you give people who have lost their minds. 'A tan.'

'Yeah, Lieutenant, a tan.' And I told him about Mrs. Radcliffe.

She had been the fifth name on my list — Mrs. John H. Radcliffe, 1272 Highland Drive, North Side. She had, according to my records, six books from the public library that were three weeks overdue. She hadn't paid any attention to our written notice, and she hadn't answered the telephone the two or three times I called her. So I went there, hoping to retrieve the books and collect the fines due on them.

It turned out to be a boxy white clapboard house in the middle of a row of seven others exactly like it; each separated from its neighbor by a narrow gravel driveway leading back, I assumed, to a garage at the rear.

I parked the Ford in front of 1272, went up the porch steps, and rang the doorbell. No answer. After waiting a few moments, I rang again. Still no answer.

After a moment's thought, I went and rang the doorbell of the house to the left. A plump lady in a dressing gown and flat bedroom slippers answered my ring at once. She had pink plastic curlers in her hair.

'Yes?' she said.

'I'm looking for the lady next door,' I replied. 'Mrs. Radcliffe. I've been trying to reach her for two weeks.'

'What do you want with her? Who are you?'

'I'm from the public library,' I explained. I showed her my ID card. 'Mrs. Radcliffe has some overdue books I'm supposed to collect.'

'In that case, I can tell you why you haven't been able to reach her. She and her husband have been in Florida for three weeks. They just got home last night.'

I had a suspicion this sharp-eyed lady was aware of most of what went on with her neighbors, so I asked, 'Do you happen to know where she or her husband are now? I'd like to get in touch with one of them.'

She nodded complacently. 'Her husband left for work at eight this morning as usual. And Dora went shopping over an hour ago.'

'Well, maybe I can stop by later this afternoon.'

'She ought to be home any minute. She goes to the supermarket around the corner.'

'In that case, I'll wait a while. Thank you very much, Mrs. — '

'Jones. And you're welcome.' She closed her door.

I went back to the car and crawled inside. The day was cold enough to see your breath, but I was quite comfortable inside the car.

After perhaps fifteen minutes a vintage Volkswagen Squareback — one where the back seats fold down flat to form a small station wagon — turned into the Radcliffe driveway and crunched over the gravel toward the back of the house, the driver giving me a curious look when she saw me parked in front of the house. The tops of numerous grocery bags showed through the rear window. I got out and followed the white car up the driveway on foot. By the time I made it to the rear, she had pulled into a rickety carport, and was already out of the VW and lifting the back panel to get at the groceries. I called to her, 'Are you Mrs. Radcliffe?'

When she turned and I saw her face, I hoped she was. She was a genuine brunette beauty with blue eyes under fine black brows and the smoothest, loveliest mahogany tan I've seen in my life. The rounded contours of her slim figure were pleasantly revealed by the slacks and windbreaker she wore.

'Yes, I'm Mrs. Radcliffe.' Her voice was as nice as her face and figure.

I introduced myself, showed her my credentials, and told her what I wanted. 'Oh,' she said with a smile, 'they're in the house. I took them to Florida with me during our vacation. I'm sorry to have caused you this trouble. If you'll wait just a minute, I'll get them for you, Mr. Johnson.'

'Let me help you carry these groceries in,' I offered. 'You have quite a load there.'

'Thanks,' she said. 'I'll open the door.' She hefted a paper bag in one arm and started for the back door. I grabbed up two more bags and followed her.

The door opened directly into the kitchen, which was small but well-equipped with modern appliances. She put her grocery bag down on the work surface between the sink and the refrigerator, and pushed a lock of shiny black hair back from her eyes. I placed my two bags beside hers and said, 'I'll get the rest of your stuff, Mrs. Radcliffe, while you get me the library books.'

'Okay,' she said, disappearing through a swinging door toward the front of the house. I returned to the Volkswagen and got the remaining bags of groceries out of the back. I was just about to slam the lid down when a glint of sunlight on metal caught my eye under a loose corner of the rubber mat that covered the VW's engine hatch.

Curious, I flipped back the mat. Lying half under its edge was a gold ring — a plain heavy band with a couple of green stones set in it. I picked it up and carried it into the house with the groceries. As I set my burden down in the kitchen, Mrs. Radcliffe's voice reached me through the swinging door: 'In here, Mr. Johnson. I've got the books.'

'Right.' I went through the swinging door and found myself in the dining area of an L-shaped living room. I rounded the corner of the L, and saw Mrs. Radcliffe depositing a stack of books on a coffee table before a gaily upholstered sofa.

'Six?' she said.

'Six is right.' I approached the coffee table, admiring the graceful curve of her back as she straightened up. 'Have you lost any gold rings lately, Mrs. Radcliffe? I found this one just now in the back of your car.' I held the ring out to her.

Her silken brows drew together in a brief puzzled frown. Then she laughed. 'Oh, *that* dumb ring! I wondered where I lost it.' She took the ring from my fingers and dropped it carelessly into a side pocket of her windbreaker. 'Thank you.'

'Dumb?' I said idly. 'It looks pretty nice to me. Almost like an antique.'

'Antique?' She laughed again, a nice little cascade of sound. 'Some antique. It's a gag gift from my husband. He gave it to me when we left for Florida.' She held out her ringless left hand. 'I don't wear a wedding ring, so Jack thought it would be fun to have me wear one on our vacation so folks would realize we were respectable married people. It was a dumb idea. And the ring was too big for me, so I promptly lost it.' She smiled at me. 'How much is the fine?'

I consulted my list. 'Six dollars and thirty cents.'

She dug into her purse, murmuring, 'Antique ring. That's good. What made you think that?'

I shrugged. 'I saw some that looked like it last winter at the Spanish Treasure Museum near Cape Kennedy, Florida. With a lot of stuff recovered from a Spanish treasure ship. Rings and bracelets and necklaces and stuff. You should have seen it. There were even some pieces of ancient Chinese porcelain.'

'Sounds fascinating,' she said. 'I'd like to see it on our next visit to Florida. This time we spent our two weeks on the west coast, near Clearwater.' She handed me a ten-dollar bill and I made change for her. Then I went through my regular routine of holding the library books upside down and riffling through them to make sure no bookmarks or forgotten papers were between the pages. A receipted bill from a Holiday Inn fell out of one of them and fluttered to the floor. I stooped over and recovered it, and handed it to Mrs. Radcliffe.

She went to open the door for me since my arms were full of books, and said, 'Thanks again, Mr. Johnson. I'm sorry I caused a bother.'

★   ★   ★

'That's it?' asked Randall when I'd finished. 'That's all? You want me to slap an attempted murder charge on Shoemaker on the basis of *that*?'

'That's just the background. It didn't mean anything to me either — until I saw the tan on Shoemaker.'

'He wasn't driving his car when it pushed you, Hal.'

'That's what he says. How do you know it's true?'

'How do I know it's not?'

'The coincidence of his having a heavy tan and owning a car that almost wasted me made me think about Mrs. Radcliffe some more. And a couple of other things that might mean something too.'

'Such as?'

'The vague impression I saw — a white Volkswagen Squareback like Mrs. Radcliffe's behind me every once in a while as I finished my morning rounds yesterday morning.'

'You think she may have been following you?'

'Maybe. I put the library books in the trunk of my car when I left her and crossed her off my list, and checked the list for my next stop. I was in front of her house long enough for her to slip into her VW and follow me if she felt like it.'

'Why should she feel like it? You're paranoid, Hal.'

I grinned at him. 'Maybe. All the same, that 'dumb' gold ring I found in her car *did* look like an honest-to-God antique, Lieutenant. Heavy yellow gold with a setting of rough-cut emeralds.'

'You couldn't tell a rough-cut emerald from a cake of green soap,' Randall hooted. 'What do you know about women's jewelry?'

'Not much. But I do know how to remember pretty good, you'll admit that, won't you?'

Randall waved a hand. 'So you've got a photographic memory. What's it got to do with this?'

'I remembered something about that hotel bill that fell out of one of Mrs. Radcliffe's library books. I didn't think anything about it at the time, but later, when these other things began to hit me — '

'What about the hotel bill?'

'It was from a Holiday Inn at Titusville, Florida.'

'And?'

'That's just a hop, skip and a jump from Cape Kennedy, where that sunken-treasure museum is.'

Randall began to look thoughtful.

'Mrs. Radcliffe told me she and her husband spent their vacation on the west coast, near Clearwater. She was lying. Why? And why did she follow me around in her car until I stopped for lunch at Johnny's Cafeteria? If she did, that is.'

Randall wasn't smiling condescendingly at me anymore. 'What time did Henderson tell you Shoemaker's car was reported stolen?'

'Twelve noon.'

'And what time did you stop for lunch at Johnny's?'

'About quarter of twelve.'

'Plenty of time for Radcliffe to telephone Shoemaker and tell him you'd seen the ring and the Holiday Inn bill. Plenty of time for him to report his car stolen before he used it to come out to Johnny's and pick up on you when you left? And maybe follow you to Wolf Hollow Bridge, where he saw his chance and pushed you off it? Is that what you mean?' When Randall's brain started ticking, it ticked fast. 'And therefore whatever Radcliffe thought you'd learned from her ring and her hotel bill was important enough to be worth killing you for?'

I said, 'I *know* what they were afraid I'd learned, Lieutenant. I went right from Haas Brothers to *The Examiner*'s office, and looked through the back copies of the newspaper for the last two weeks. I found this item that I missed when it came out last week.' I put the copy I'd made of it down on the desk before him. It had an inconspicuous two-column headline followed by a brief block of text. It had been on page 4 of the first section four days ago.

GUARD SLAIN IN MILLION-DOLLAR ROBBERY

Cape Kennedy (UP) Police intensified their search today for the thieves who fatally shot a museum guard while stealing nearly a million dollars' worth of old coins and jewelry from the Museum of Spanish Treasure here last Friday.

Cape Kennedy Police Chief George Boniface said he had alerted smelting firms throughout Florida about the theft, hoping to head off any attempt to melt down the irreplaceable artifacts.

The thieves broke into the museum early Friday morning, bypassed burglar alarms with apparent ease, smashed plate-glass display cases, and helped themselves to the eighteenth-century Spanish treasure recovered from the sea floor.

The lone security guard on duty,

Lancelot Frederick, was shot by one of the thieves when he attempted to prevent the robbery. He later succumbed after informing police there were two men and a woman involved in the theft, all wearing ski masks to conceal their identities.

Lieutenant Randall didn't bother to read the item all the way through. He grabbed the phone and barked into the mouthpiece, 'Get me the Police Chief of Cape Kennedy, Florida, Jerry, name of George Boniface — in a hurry!' He turned toward me, slamming the receiver down. 'We'll take it from here, Hal. I'll be in touch.'

I stood up. 'Go easy on Mrs. Radcliffe,' I said. 'I feel like a heel for even suspecting her.'

* * *

A few weeks later, the affair had been wrapped up with Randall's usual neatness and dispatch. Shoemaker and the Radcliffes had been returned to Florida to stand trial for murder, armed robbery, and grand theft, with enough solid evidence to put them away for a long, long time.

Item: Shoemaker's Police Positive .38 revolver, which was found to have fired the bullet that ended the life of the museum guard. Item: a penciled diagram of the intricate burglar-alarm system of the Spanish Treasure Museum, obviously made on the spot during preliminary visits to the museum by John Radcliffe, who turned out to be not only an electrical engineer employed by a local firm called Continental Alarms, Inc., but a college classmate and the oldest friend of Frank Shoemaker. Item: a taped confession by Mrs. Radcliffe, recounting the robbery and designating Frank Shoemaker as the guard's killer. And item: two suitcases full of the Spanish treasure stolen from the museum, discovered by police in the bedroom closet of Frank Shoemaker at 818 Northway Road.

I told Ellen all about it over dinner at the Lotus Bud, one of the poshest restaurants around. I was mellow enough from two martinis and a half bottle of Mateus rosé to boast a little. 'Aren't you proud of me, Ellen?' I asked her. 'Figuring out the entire plot from a ring they just happened to drop when they were stowing their loot in the back of Radcliffe's VW for their trip home?'

She said, 'Of course I'm proud of you. But they almost *killed* you, Hal.'

'Would you have cared?'

'Of course.' She flashed me a smile. 'It would have been very bad publicity for the library.'

'Well,' I said, sighing, 'that brings me to the reason I've told you all this. The Florida authorities were so glad to get their treasure back and catch the thieves, they suggested a small reward might be in order for the alert, honest library fuzz who solved the case for them.'

'A reward!' Ellen exclaimed. 'How exciting! What is it?'

'I have it right here in my pocket.' I pulled out the antique gold ring I'd found in the back of Mrs. Radcliffe's car. The dull-gold band looked bright and polished under the restaurant lights; the rough-cut emeralds glistened. I held it out to Ellen.

She took it and said, 'Oh, how lovely,' and turned it this way and that, tilting her head to examine it from different angles. At last, she said, 'It's very beautiful, Hal, but what in the world do they think you're going to do with a fancy thing like this, a man of your simple ascetic tastes?'

I shrugged. 'It would make a nice wedding ring,' I suggested.

'For me?'

'For you.'

She slipped it on her ring finger. 'It's too big for me.'

'I'll have it made smaller.'

She protested, 'It would cost us a fortune to waste any of this gold.'

Cost *us*? My heart began to hammer. 'Does that mean you'll take it?'

She said, 'Is Mrs. Radcliffe really all that gorgeous?'

'A knockout,' I said. 'A dish. Black hair, blue eyes. With that sexy tan, she's the best-looking woman I've seen in my life. Except for you.'

'I could wear the ring around my neck

on a chain,' Ellen said. 'Would that be all right with you, Hal?'

I took a deep breath and my cracked rib responded with a brief stab of pain. 'Wear it anywhere you want to,' I said, 'just as long as you wear it.'

She leaned over and kissed me, ignoring the other diners around us. I felt a wave of euphoria wash over me — a blessed mixture of triumph, love, tenderness. 'Are you saying we're engaged?' I said, having trouble with my voice.

'You better believe it,' said Ellen.

9

The Book Clue

It wasn't one of your ordinary hit-and-run, in-and-out bank robberies.

It was, in fact, a real work of art, a model from which any earnest young apprentice in the bank-robbing trade could have learned plenty.

It took place over the frigid New Year's weekend — a three-day holiday, since New Year's Day fell on Saturday — so the thieves had three full days and nights to knock a hole through the rear wall of the bank, disarm the bank's elaborate alarm system, cut open the vault with acetylene torches, and rifle through the contents of two hundred private safe-deposit boxes.

Later, when the owners of the stolen valuables came to the bank and reported the extent of their losses, the bank estimated that the thieves had made off with roughly three and a half million dollars' worth of cash, securities, jewelry, antiques, coin collections, and whatnot.

Not a bad haul for three days' work — especially since the looters made a clean getaway, leaving behind them — aside from the shambles of empty deposit boxes and a hole in the wall — only a few traces of their three-day visit. A small pile of rubble from the shattered wall. A thin film of plaster dust on the floor of the bank inside the hole, marked with hundreds of indecipherable footprints. Scattered crumbs of crackers and cheese and some coffee splashes on the vault floor. The crusts of several peanut-butter sandwiches on the vault custodian's desk. And nothing else. Except for embarrassed bankers, puzzled policemen, and rueful insurance adjusters.

About noon on the fourth of January, I was at my desk at the Central Library working on my next overdue list, when the girl on the switchboard rang through and said a police officer wanted to talk to me.

'Lieutenant Randall?' I asked. Randall

was Chief of Homicide, and had been my boss for five years before I joined the Public Library staff.

'No, Hal. Somebody named Waslyck.'

Waslyck, Head of the Robbery Detail. Jake Waslyck. Sure, I remembered him from the old days. 'Put him on,' I said.

'Hal?' His voice came through like gravel on a tin roof. 'How you doing, Hal?'

'Can't complain, Jake. You?'

'I can complain,' he said. 'Plenty.'

'The First Federal Bank job, right? I read about it in the papers.'

'Who didn't? I want to ask a favor of you, Hal.'

'Any time,' I said. 'What?'

'I need advice. Can you stop in here or shall I come out there?'

'I'll be downtown this afternoon. I'll stop by headquarters. Advice about what?'

'One of your library books. See you about three?'

'Two-thirty would suit me better.'

'See you then.'

★ ★ ★

241

At two-thirty, I was in Jake's office. The place is cramped, smells strongly of stale cigar smoke, and is furnished in police-station modern: a battered steel desk, worn linoleum on the floor, a scratched filing cabinet in one corner, an old-fashioned hat rack in another, two uncomfortable straight-backed chairs, and a grimy Venetian blind over the unwashed window.

Jake sat behind his desk, his squat body overflowing his chair, his bulgy eyes red and puffy. His bushy ginger mustache was badly in need of trimming. And he didn't seem to have any neck at all.

Same old Jake. He looked a lot like an oversized bullfrog crouching there. But I remembered there was nothing wrong with his brain.

I sat down gingerly in one of his straight chairs. It trembled under my weight as I reached across the desk to shake hands. I said, not entirely sincerely, 'Nice to see you again, Jake. It's been a while.'

In a frog's croak of a voice, he said, 'Thanks for coming in, Hal.' He paused.

'You look shot,' I said. 'The First Federal job getting to you?'

He nodded. 'We got nothing to go on. ID's still comparing fingerprints, trying to find some that aren't those of safe-deposit box holders or bank custodians. Absolutely no luck so far.'

'It's probably hopeless,' I said sympathetically. 'It was below zero that weekend. They needed gloves, for the cold if nothing else.'

'Yeah. So we got zilch. No leads. No suspects. We're going around in circles on a three-million-dollar robbery!' He cleared his throat. 'It's a hell of a feeling, believe me.'

'Frustration,' I said. 'I know what you mean, Jake. I've been there.'

'So that's why I called you. I'm clutching at straws.'

'Like the library book you mentioned?'

He gave one sharp nod, up and down. 'Tell me about it.'

'It's a book we found in our search of the bank vault after the heist. You know those little booths where they let you gloat over your treasures in private?'

'Yeah.'

'Well, we found this book from your

library under the table in one of those booths.'

'And you think it's a *clue*, maybe?' I underlined the 'clue' with my voice. Cops hate the word.

'Not really. But a million-to-one chance. See, we figured, considering where the book was found and all, that some box-holder had left it in the booth by mistake when he stopped in last week to count his fortune or whatever.'

'Doesn't the vault custodian always come in afterward and check out the booth to see you haven't left anything behind? Mine always does.'

Jake said, deadpan, 'You mean you rent a safe-deposit box?'

'Sure. But not at First Federal, thank God.'

'What do you keep in it?' He was needling me.

'I skim a little off the top of the fines I collect.'

'That must come to — let's see, maybe forty cents a week?'

'In a good week,' I said. We both laughed. My laugh had a little edge in it,

I'm afraid. 'You're saying that a vault custodian might not notice a library book under a booth table?'

'It's possible. Those guards are only checking the booth to see if you've left a thousand shares of IBM or something like that lying around.'

'So?'

'So last night when I couldn't sleep, it suddenly occurred to me that the library book just possibly might be something the *thieves* took into the vault when they broke in.'

'You mean, so they'd have something to read during coffee breaks?' The idea tickled me.

'Why not? They're in there for three days and nights, remember. They bring in cheese and crackers, thermoses of hot coffee, sandwiches — we even found some bits of fabric the lab says could be from a sleeping-bag lining. So why not something to read during their rest periods? Maybe one of them is a book nut. You know, keen on books.'

'It's a long shot,' I said, grinning. 'But possible, I suppose. Let's see the book.'

Jake yelled 'Josie!' at the top of his voice, and a minute later Detective Second-Class Josie Evans came into his office from the squad room across the hall. I remembered Josie from old times, too. She's black, slender, and very attractive in her navy-blue skirt and white blouse. To look at her you'd never guess she can toss a two-hundred-pound man over her shoulder without even mussing her hair.

She recognized me. 'Hi, Hal,' she said.

I said, 'Hi, Josie. What's a nice girl like you doing in a place like this?'

'Defending my virtue, most of the time,' she answered tartly. 'What is it, Jake?'

'Bring me the library book we found in the bank vault.' He turned to me. 'Josie's a book nut, too. She's reading the damn thing.'

'I've finished it,' Josie said. 'It's a swell story.' She went out, and returned shortly with it. After she left, I said to Jake, 'You think this book may be evidence in the biggest bank robbery this state ever had, and you're letting Josie *read* it, for God's sake?'

'Relax, Hal. Relax. The book's been put through the works by the lab already and gives us nothing. Except about two hundred sets of smudged latents from former readers. That's why I asked you to come in. Maybe you can get more from it than we can.'

I picked up the book. 'It's from our Central Library.'

'I can read, Hal. I saw the stamp.'

'There's no return card in the pocket.'

'I noticed that, too.'

I grinned at him. 'And furthermore,' I said, not averse to needling *him* a little, 'it's a hell of a good yarn, like Josie said — ' The book was a popular novel by Wilbur Smith called *The Eye of the Tiger*. ' — just like the old-time goodies by H. Rider Haggard.'

Waslyck grunted. 'Can you find out who borrowed the book from the library?'

'Sure. Name, address, and library-card number. Simple. Our computer coughs that stuff up on demand. But — ' I held up a hand as he started to speak. ' — wait a minute, Jake.' Another small jab of the needle wouldn't hurt, I thought. I had it on good authority that Jake Waslyck was one of my many former colleagues in the police department who had been known to refer to me slightingly as Library Fuzz Hal, the sissy ex-Homicide cop who now spent his time tracking down library books instead of murderers ... and although this was perfectly true, I didn't like them patronizing me. My work's a lot quieter than theirs, it pays just as well, and I can sleep better at night. So I said, 'Our computer coughs up what you want only if the book happens to be overdue.'

'Why the hell's that?'

'Invasion of privacy,' I said. 'Until a book is overdue, it legally belongs to the borrower. Our library is a *public* library. It's none of our business who has a book until it goes overdue. Then it belongs to us again.'

Waslyck swore. 'Listen, this is an official request from a police officer — a *public servant* — for the name and address of a suspect who may have been involved in the commission of a major felony.' He glared at me.

I smiled. 'In that case, our computer

might be conned into making an exception. You see, Jake, we have this nifty secret code to bypass our computer's compunctions about breaking the privacy laws. We feed in the first three letters of the author's name — his last name — then we feed in the middle two digits of the book's Zebra patch number. Then comes the middle initial of the city's current Democratic mayor — '

'Knock it off, Hal. This is serious. Can you get me the information I want?'

'I'll try.' I stood up. 'I'll have to take the book with me, okay?'

He made a dismissive gesture. I took the book and left.

I called him back within half an hour. 'I've got it,' I said. 'The book *is* overdue. You ready?'

'Shoot.'

'The address is 1221 Bookbinders Lane.'

He wrote it down. 'What's the name?'

'You won't like this, Jake. The name is Adelaide Westover.'

Jake swore. 'A woman!'

'Seems like it,' I said. 'I'm sorry. It kind of blows your theory, doesn't it?'

'Not necessarily,' said Jake, but his disappointment was evident in his tone. 'I've heard of woman bank robbers before. Like Clyde's lady friend, Bonnie.'

Trying to cheer him up, I said, 'This Adelaide Westover may have wanted to spend the long weekend with *her* boyfriend, so she went along with him on the bank job and curled up with a good book while he worked.'

Waslyck ignored that. After a moment's silence, he said, 'I think we'll give it a whirl anyway, Hal. We might get lucky.'

★ ★ ★

Ten minutes later, my phone rang, and it was Jake Waslyck. He said harshly, 'You sure that's the name and address your computer came up with?'

'Sure I'm sure.'

'Then your computer has a slipped disk. There's no such street as Bookbinders Lane in this city or any of its suburbs. And there's no such person as Adelaide Westover listed in the City Directory or the phonebook.'

I sighed. 'Then the book was borrowed on a phony card, Jake — a card issued to a fictitious person at a fictitious address. Sometimes people lie about their names and addresses when they apply for a library card, and show us fake references. We can't check up on every citizen who applies for a card. But it doesn't happen often.'

'I thought it was your job to prevent that sort of thing.'

'It is. I'll see what I can do about this. If I come up with anything, I'll let you know, Jake . . . '

Four days later, I telephoned Waslyck. It was around five o'clock in the afternoon and he'd gone off duty. I called him at home.

His wife answered the phone. 'Hello?' she said, in a rich creamy contralto that made me wonder how she ever came to marry a cop with a voice like a bullfrog.

'I'd like to speak to Jake if he's there,' I said.

'Who's calling?'

'Hal Johnson from the public library.'

'Hold on.'

'Hi,' he said when he came on the line.

I said, 'I think I've got something for you on that library book, Jake. It's too complicated for the telephone. I better see you.'

'Okay. Be in my office at noon tomorrow.'

'Right,' I said. I hung up, feeling unappreciated and put-upon.

*　*　*

I was in his office at noon, sitting on the same shaky chair. Jake greeted me with a short question.

'What you got?'

'Well, our library thief might possibly — just possibly — have something to do with *your* problem. I think I'm on to his real identity. But I'm not sure. I need your advice this time.'

Waslyck sat back in his creaking swivel chair. 'Make it short. Okay?'

I said, 'I questioned all the check-out people at Central Library about Adelaide Westover. Did anybody remember anybody checking out a book called *The Eye of the Tiger* by Wilbur Smith on a card made out in that name on that date? It didn't have to be a woman. Nobody remembered anything.'

'Figures,' said Jake.

'So then I thought, what if this Adelaide Westover, whoever she really is, borrowed other books by Wilbur Smith with her phony library card? Your library card is good,' I explained parenthetically, 'at any of our branches. And you can return borrowed books to any branch you want to. Did you know that, Jake?'

'To my shame, I didn't.' Jake tapped his fingers impatiently on his desk.

'Well, I checked out all our Wilbur Smith titles, both at Central and all our branches — no easy job, since Smith has had six or eight successful books published in this country, and some of our branches have as many as six copies of each one circulating. Thank God for our computer.'

Jake said an unpleasant word.

I went on blithely, 'Which is how I found out that three other Smith titles have gone overdue — although not long enough overdue to have been brought to my attention just yet.'

Jake was following me closely now. 'And the three overdue Smith books were checked out to Adelaide Westover?' he guessed.

'No, only one of them. A book called *The Delta Decision*. The other two titles — *A Sparrow Falls* and *Hungry As the Sea* — were checked out at our North Side and East Gate branches by two different people entirely. The book from North Side branch was checked out to Alexander Warfield. 15101 Quarto Avenue; the book from East Gate was checked out to Alan Woolfolk, who supposedly resides at 6225 Doubleday Drive.'

'But doesn't?'

'But doesn't. Nor does any Alexander Warfield reside at 15101 Quarto Avenue. There are no such people and no such addresses in the city.'

'More phony library cards?'

'Seems like.'

Jake mulled it over for a few seconds. 'And you figure the three phony library patrons are one and the same person?

Because they all borrowed Smith's books?'

I nodded. 'Sometimes people borrow a book by an author they've never tried before, and they like it so much they want to read all the other books the author has written.'

'And this joker who uses fake library cards has gone ape over Wilbur Smith.'

I shrugged. 'Could be. If the three phony names and addresses are the same person.'

'You think they are?'

'Yeah,' I said.

'Why?'

'Look at the names.' I passed him my notebook. 'Look at the addresses.'

'The names have the same initials — Adelaide Westover, Alexander Warfield, Alan Woolfolk.'

'Right. And, as I remember from my Homicide work, a lot of people use their own initials when they're dreaming up an alias.'

'Are you saying your book borrower's real initials are A.W.?'

'It seems reasonable.'

'I'll buy that. But what about the addresses?'

'All three street names have something

to do with books. The kind of phony names a guy who likes books might come up with. Bookbinders Lane. Quarto Avenue. Doubleday Drive.'

'Okay. So what's the phony's real name, then?' Waslyck leaned forward in his chair.

'Don't you want to hear how I nosed him out?' I asked innocently.

'No, I don't. But you're going to tell me anyway.'

'All three phony library cards were issued at our South Side branch,' I said. 'That narrowed things down. But naturally nobody at South Side remembered anything about issuing them, so I pulled the application files of all the library volunteers who work at South Side and are authorized by our librarian to issue new library cards. Did you know we have twenty-seven volunteers working an average of four hours a week without pay at the South Side branch?'

'I know it now.'

'So, after examining the applications of volunteers over the past few years at South Side, I talked with the librarian and her assistant — and came up with a really hot-looking suspect for you.'

'Who?' asked Jake.

'A volunteer named Arthur West. Sixty-nine years old, authority to issue new library cards, ready access to the check-out and check-in machines, considered a compulsive reader by his associates. He works twelve hours a week at our South Side branch without pay, has a pleasant personality, a minuscule income from Social Security, and a negligible pension from his former employers.'

Waslyck interrupted, 'But what's this Arthur West got to do with the First Federal Bank job?'

'That's what I wanted to ask your advice about,' I said. 'He's got a small checking account at First Federal, for one thing.'

'So have hundreds of other people.'

'Our South Side branch is right next door to the bank.'

That got me nothing but a blank look.

'Arthur West often brings his lunch to the library in a paper bag — and the lunch invariably consists of peanut-butter sandwiches.'

'Half the people in the world eat peanut-butter sandwiches for lunch,' Jake said wearily.

'But Arthur West doesn't eat his crusts,' I said. 'Just like one of your bank robbers.'

'The world's full of people who don't eat their crusts.'

'True, Lieutenant,' I said, 'but the world's *not* full of library volunteers whose names begin with the letters A and W, who are peanut-butter-sandwich fiends who don't eat their crusts, who are living on inadequate incomes, and who — ' I paused for dramatic effect. ' — were employed before their retirement by the Universal Security Company of Chicago, whose specialty is the manufacture and installation of sophisticated alarm systems for banks.'

Waslyck acted as though a bomb had exploded under his chair. He shot to his feet. 'Why the hell didn't you tell me that in the first place? Where can I find this Arthur West? You *do* know *his* address, I take it?'

'He lives in a rented room over The Corner Cupboard Bar and Grill out in

Lake Point. You know The Corner Cupboard, Lieutenant?'

'Who doesn't? It's a dive. Some very hard characters hang out there.'

'Well, that's where Arthur West does his beer-drinking and eats most of his dinners,' I said. 'And maybe it's where he recruited his help for the bank job.'

Waslyck yelled for Josie. When she showed up in the doorway, he said, 'Get your coat on and check out a car for us — I'll meet you down in the garage.' He took his own overcoat off the hat rack in the corner. The thermometer was still flirting with zero outside.

I said, 'Aren't you going to get a search warrant before you go out there? You want to keep things legal, don't you?'

Jake gave me an exasperated look. 'You know something, Hal?' he asked. 'I'm really glad you don't work here anymore.' He turned for the door. 'So now get lost, will you? I'll let you know how this turns out.'

★ ★ ★

The morning newspaper next day told me all I needed to know — under a front-page headline. The police, the story went, acting on a tip from an informer, had arrested an elderly man named Arthur West in The Corner Cupboard Bar and Grill the previous afternoon and charged him with complicity in the sensational robbery, ten days ago, of First Federal Bank on the South Side. According to police Lieutenant Jacob Waslyck, other arrests were imminent. A search of West's rented room above the bar led to the recovery of almost a third of the loot stolen from First Federal's safe-deposit vault. The stolen valuables had been found hidden in a sleeping bag under West's daybed. The police reported that West's room also contained seven hundred and forty-two books bearing the identification stamp and card pockets of books from the Public Library.

That last item, I knew, was a direct message from Lieutenant Waslyck to me. His way of saying thanks — or a malicious reminder that I wasn't any better at my job than he was at his.

* * *

I found a message on my desk when I got to the library that morning. Dr. Forbes, the Library Director, wanted to see me in his office right away. His spacious office is right next to my cubbyhole. He could have yelled for me, and usually does. But this morning the message was formal. Dr. Forbes must be upset. And I thought I knew why.

He looked at me over the newspaper he was reading. Before he could say anything, I blurted out, 'Dr. Forbes, I know what you're thinking and I don't blame you. But that newspaper article didn't mention two important facts. One, that Arthur West, the bank robber and library-book thief, is also a trusted volunteer who works at our South Side branch. And two, the informant who tipped off the police to him was me.'

His expression went from stormy to partly cloudy. 'Tell me about it, Hal,' he said.

I told him everything. When I finished, his expression had gone from partly cloudy to fair and warmer. He said, 'No wonder we didn't realize the books were missing. West checked them out to himself on spurious cards, and before they were overdue he checked the cards back in again without actually returning the books.'

'Exactly. We were lucky he forgot to check those Smith titles in before they showed up as overdue on our computer.'

'Why do you suppose he forgot to do it?'

'Maybe he was too busy planning the bank robbery — or, more likely, after over seven hundred book thefts, he began to think his system was foolproof and we'd never get on to him. He got careless.'

Dr. Forbes smiled.

'So am I fired, or not?' I ventured to ask him.

'Not,' he said.

★   ★   ★

Two weeks went by. Two weeks during which I carried out my duties as usual. Two weeks during which Arthur West plea-bargained himself down to a charge of petty book theft in return for naming his accomplices in the bank robbery and agreeing to testify against them when their trials came up. Two weeks during which said accomplices — an apprentice plumber and a backhoe operator, both local citizens and regular patrons of The Corner Cupboard Bar and Grill — were duly charged with bank robbery. Two weeks during which, to everyone's relief, the other two-thirds of the missing loot was recovered almost intact: the plumber's share from a beat-up suitcase in a locker at the Greyhound Bus Station; the backhoe man's zipped into one of his wife's drip-dry pillow-covers, and stashed in the crawlspace between his garage ceiling and roof.

On Saturday night of the second week, I took Ellen Thomas out to dinner at Jimmy's Crab House. Ellen is the girl who holds down the check-out desk at the Central Library. She has promised to marry me as soon as we can acquire an adequate nest-egg to see us through any rainy days in the future.

We were facing each other across a narrow table in a booth. Ellen looked at the prices on the menu and said, 'Are you out of your mind, Hal? This place is too fancy for us.'

I said, 'I'm going to have Maine lobster, myself.'

'Maine lobster?' She hesitated. 'If you say so.' Another pause. 'Me, too.'

The waiter took our orders and in due course brought in the lobsters. They were delicious. Not worth the price, but delicious.

Between bites, Ellen said, 'What's the occasion, Hal? It is one, isn't it?' She gave me her up-from-under keen look.

'Yeah,' I said, 'a celebration of sorts.'

'What sort? A celebration of what?'

'Wait till dessert,' I said. 'I want to surprise you.'

'Okay. I'll wait.' She worked on her lobster for a bit. Then she said, 'I can't wait any longer, Hal. Tell me now. Why are we blowing a week's wages at this elegant restaurant?'

'Because,' I replied, 'the First Federal and their insurance people got together and decided to give the Police Benevolent Fund and Hal Johnson from the Public Library a small reward in recognition of their services in solving the robbery and recovering their loot.'

'Hey!' cried Ellen, her eyes shining. 'My hero! How much?'

'Ten thousand for the PBF, ten thousand for me.'

She was stunned. She stared at me, her eyes wide with outrage. 'Ten thousand dollars,' she said indignantly. 'Ten thousand dollars for saving them three and a half million!'

I agreed. 'But ten thousand is better than nothing.'

She brightened.

'It's pretty wonderful when you think about it. We've got our nest-egg in one fell swoop. Now we can get married.'

I said, 'On ten thousand dollars? You call that a nest-egg? It's hardly enough for a decent honeymoon. Not nearly enough to pay the obstetrician for the sixteen children we're going to have. Think of the college tuition for only one of the sixteen.' I shook my head. 'No way, Ellen. Suppose

I lose my job or you lose yours? Suppose one of us has to spend a couple of weeks in a hospital sometime? Or we get divorced and I have to pay alimony and child support? Where would the money come from?'

Ellen leaned across the table and gave me a buttery kiss. 'Well,' she said, 'we could always rob a bank, couldn't we?'